MW00653113

THE FIELDS OF LEMURIA

(SEQUEL TO THE WALLS OF LEMURIA)

SAM SISAVATH

The Fields of Lemuria
Copyright © 2014 by Sam Sisavath

All rights reserved.

No part of this publication may be reproduced, distributed, or transmitted in any form or by any means, including photocopying, recording, or other electronic or mechanical methods, without the prior written permission of the publisher, except in the case of brief quotations embodied in critical reviews and certain other noncommercial uses permitted by copyright law.

Disclaimer: This is a work of fiction. Names, characters, businesses, places, events and incidents are either the products of the author's imagination or used in a fictitious manner. Any resemblance to actual persons, living or dead, or actual events is purely coincidental.

Published by Road to Babylon Media
www.roadtobabylon.com

Edited by Jennifer Jensen & Wendy Chan
Cover Art by Creative Paramita
Formatting by BB eBooks

ISBN-13: 978-0692285909
ISBN-10: 0692285903

Books in the Ongoing *Babylon* Series
(Reading Order)

The Purge of Babylon
The Gates of Byzantium
The Stones of Angkor
The Fires of Atlantis

Books in the Stand-Alone
Purge of Babylon: Lemuria Series

The Walls of Lemuria

And now…

The Fields of Lemuria

Thank you to all the readers who have followed me on this journey so far. Five books into the series and your enthusiasm keeps me pounding away at the keyboard. Truly, none of this would be possible without your adventurous spirit. You took a chance on a nobody, and for that I'm forever grateful.

"Who the hell are these guys?"

Hunted through the Louisiana woods by a mysterious paramilitary group, Keo and Norris are about to reach the end of the line.

After months of running, hiding, and fighting for their lives, the ex-mercenary and the ex-cop will finally discover the identity of their pursuers—and why they will never, ever give up.

The planet may have been purged and the ghouls now hold complete dominion over the night, but in the day, man still remains the deadliest species.

After the Walls come down, the Fields will run red with blood...

NOTE: This is the direct sequel to The Walls of Lemuria and leads into the events of The Fires of Atlantis (Book 4 in the ongoing Purge of Babylon series).

PART ONE

THE CRUCIBLE

CHAPTER 1

"HOW MANY OF you are out there?" he had asked the man named Doug.

"A lot," Doug had answered.

That man was dead, and Keo had already killed three more of Doug's friends since the house gun battle that had separated him from Gillian and the others. Not that it had slowed the rest of Doug's friends for even a single day. Which made him wonder how many of them there actually were.

A dozen? Two? A *hundred?*

How many was *"a lot"?*

Before he knew it, he and Norris were moving through the woods of Louisiana again. By now, they had lost sight of the river completely, and their only option was to continue south. Somewhere down there was Baton Rouge and New Orleans. And beyond that was *(Gillian)* the Gulf of Mexico. All they had to do was keep moving south.

That was easier said than done.

They ended up at Robertson Park, a long stretch of wooded area shaped like a cone, getting smaller the farther south you went, and flanked to the east, west, and south by a landlocked body of water called Downey Creek Lake. He only knew where they were because of the signs along the roads, though he didn't have a clue what part of the state it was exactly, or if a town or city was nearby. They had lost their map more than two months ago during a skirmish that nearly cost Norris his life and were essentially moving blind, pushed forward by the men in black assault vests. At times Keo thought he and Norris were being herded, purposefully directed down here. But that couldn't have been possible.

Could it?

Who the hell are these guys?

Robertson Park was big enough that it took them most of the day moving from end to end before they realized the only way out was to double back north. While they were attempting to circumvent the area, Keo noticed one thing that struck him as strange: the docks along the shoreline were empty. He didn't spot a single boat they could have used—not even a dinghy raft to paddle their way to the other side of the lake.

Where did all the boats go?

The question nagged at him throughout the day, but he soon forgot about it because there were more immediate and important things to worry about. Whenever his thoughts drifted, there was always something to drag him back to the present.

Like food. Water. Or trying to stay out of another ambush...

Crossing the lake was out of the question, so they had to do it the hard way. Which was nothing new. It had been the only way for over two months now. Or was it more than that? They hadn't been in the woods for three months, had they? No. That was impossible. It was probably just two months. Or two and a half months.

Probably.

The nights had a way of blending together, and neither he nor Norris were actually keeping tabs on the days anymore. They didn't know their Mondays from their Fridays from their weekends. Not that it mattered. One day was the same as the other, taken up with the constant search for shelter. Those were the good days. The bad ones usually involved a lot of running, hiding, and fighting. Always fighting.

The problem with doubling back out of the park was the men pursuing them. By now, he was pretty sure they had tracked them into Robertson and were pushing him and Norris south toward the tip. The woods were longer than they were wide, so it didn't take a lot of men to create a staggering wall. God knew they had plenty of men.

"How many of you are out there?"

"A lot."

They were halfway back to the park entrance when they caught sight of their pursuers, men in black assault vests armed with assault rifles and carrying what seemed like more ammo than God himself.

Where the hell did they get all the ammo?

He and Norris didn't even have to talk about it. They just turned around and began moving south again.

Their one advantage—their *only* advantage—was that the massive center of Robertson Park consisted of hundreds of wooded acres containing densely packed trees, underbrush, and nothing resembling civilization. Once upon a time, there had been a lot of wildlife in here, and hunters roamed freely. Those days were long gone, though. Unlike the middle, the shorelines had been developed for human habitation with a string of high-priced homes, each one complete with private boat docks. *(What happened to all the boats?)*

With the exit denied them, Keo and Norris retreated back to a lakeside house on the southeast side. The house had two stories, with a large window on the second floor that gave them a great view of the surrounding area. If their pursuers showed up, they would be approaching from the north. The window would give them a minor advantage, but right now he would take anything he could get.

The house, like all the others in the area they had scavenged for food and supplies, was devoid of signs anyone had lived in it since November of last year. Thin layers of dust covered the furniture and tiles, and the beds on the second floor were undisturbed. It was like walking into a museum, a "This is How the Rich and Famous Lived in the 21st Century" tableau.

He heard footsteps now as Norris came up the carpeted stairs behind him. The fifty-six-year-old ex-cop from Orlando was already breathing hard by the time he reached the top. "Jesus, did you have to pick a two-story house?"

"Stop your complaining," Keo said. "Murtaugh wouldn't complain this much."

"Murtaugh would complain so much you'd want to shoot him in the back of the head while he slept."

"You're getting there."

Norris snorted. He walked over to the window and slid against the wall on the other side and peered out.

If Keo thought the trees looked massive from the ground, he got a better sense of their towering height from the second floor of the house. They stood tall, the crowns hovering over them still. It was quiet outside, the only noise coming from the chirping birds and the scraping of claws from two squirrels racing across a branch directly in front of them. Those were the only animals that were safe these days—the ones small and fast enough to escape into the trees when *they* came out at night.

"They out there?" Norris asked.

"I don't see anything."

"Maybe we lost them."

"Maybe you're daydreaming again."

Norris grunted. "Maybe you're right."

The older man pulled a bottle of water from the backpack slung over his back. The tactical pack, along with the spare magazines in the pouches around his waist, were courtesy of the men they had killed. Keo carried his own "collected" pack and ammo, but he had run out of bullets for the MP5SD two weeks ago. Although he was now relying on a beat-up M4 that its former owner no longer needed, he still kept the submachine gun in a sling over his back. You never knew when you would run across some 9mm rounds just lying around. He was in the South, after all. Ammo and guns tended to be plentiful down here.

"We're running low," Norris said, holding out the bottle to him.

"So what else is new?" Keo said, taking the proffered bottle.

Like most of the houses they had searched in the last few days, there wasn't a single unopened bottle of water, non-perishable food, or weapon to be found. There were plenty of knives, but there were only so many sharp things you could carry around with you. What he wouldn't have given for a can of fruit, or sardines, or saltine crackers.

Boats are gone. So are the supplies. Someone's living off the park. So where are they?

Norris had come to the same conclusion, but they hadn't spent another second wondering where those people were. It didn't matter. Like always, they had other, more immediate concerns. Like the men in black assault vests pushing south toward them…

He drank half of the water bottle and poured the rest over his head and face in an attempt to wash the dirt and grime off him. If how he felt afterward as the water rolled off him and onto the carpeting was any indication, it didn't work.

Norris gave him a disapproving look. "If you were my kid, I'd slap you across the face for wasting water."

Keo grinned. "If I was your kid, I'd slap myself."

Norris smirked. "Smartass."

"You never told me why you never had any kids."

"Why didn't you ever have any kids?"

"I didn't think I was going to live this long. What's your excuse?"

"Seriously, kid, for a guy who keeps telling me he doesn't expect to see his thirtieth birthday, you're sure good at all this surviving stuff."

Keo shrugged. "It's a bad habit."

The fact was, Norris could easily be his father. The retiree had twenty-eight years on him, and all of it showed on his heavily-lined face and gray beard at the moment. Norris hadn't always looked as old as he did now, but constantly running for his life from men with assault rifles in the day while hiding from undead things during the night hadn't done him any favors.

Like Keo, Norris was covered in old and new dirt, and drying and still-wet mud caked their shoes along with their sweat-stained shirts and pants. How long had they been wearing the same clothes now? He couldn't even start to guess. Wardrobe changes hadn't been a priority for either one of them in a long time.

Keo tossed the bottle across the room's luxury carpeting. Every inch of the lakeside house screamed money. Mid six figures if he was lowballing it, but probably somewhere in the seven figures. There were pictures of a family along the front hallway when they entered, but Keo made an effort not to look. He disliked staring at the frozen and happy faces of people who were probably dead *(or worse)*.

"How's your leg?" he asked Norris.

"Bummed," Norris said, looking out the window.

"What does that mean?"

"It hurts; what do you think it means?"

"Well, you were only shot once, so be grateful. I'm lugging around two bullet holes here."

"Should learn to duck better, kid," Norris grinned.

Keo grunted back. Norris had been shot in the thigh not all that long ago, and despite his self-prognosis, he seemed to be moving much better in recent weeks. Keo had two bullet holes in him—one in the left shoulder and the other in the right leg. They throbbed whenever he moved any part of his body, and pretending they didn't had stopped working about three weeks earlier. The ironic part was that the only time he didn't feel the pain was whenever he was running, something he was doing a lot of these days. At nights, though, when they found a place to hide, it was impossible not to remember he had been shot while fleeing from the same group of men hunting them now.

Who the hell are these guys?

"How long do you think they're going to keep this up?" Norris asked. He hadn't looked away once from the window in the last ten minutes.

"I don't know," Keo said. "If they didn't give up after the house, I don't think they're going to give up now."

"How many have we killed since? Three?"

"Yeah. I got two, and you got the last one."

"You sure I didn't get the second one, too?"

"I'm pretty sure."

"I don't believe you. You wouldn't lie to an old man, would you?"

"Absolutely," Keo smiled. "It's not like I actually respect you—"

Pak!

A bullet drilled through the glass between the two of them. The round kept going, slicing across the room before slamming into the wall on the other side.

Keo pulled his head back, Norris doing the same across the window.

He hadn't heard the gunshot, which meant they were using a silenced rifle. That was new. When had they resorted to that? Keo was so used to the loud rattle of gunfire that the soundless bullet shocked him for just a moment. It didn't last long, though, and his survival instincts quickly kicked in.

"Downstairs!" he shouted, racing to the stairs.

Pak-pak-pak!

More bullets smashed through the window behind him, chipping away glass and frame and embedding into the wallpaper over his head. Keo didn't spend too much time worrying about Norris. The ex-cop had proven himself more than capable in a gunfight. They had saved each other's lives more times than Keo cared to count, so when he left Norris on the second floor, he knew the older man would do his job just fine.

He jumped the last four steps to the bottom. It was a stupid move, and he regretted it right away even while he was still in mid-air, because even though he had prepared himself for the jolt of pain that was coming *(You idiot, remember the bullet hole in the leg?)* it still managed to catch him by surprise.

Keo almost lost his footing as he landed and stumbled, sticking out the M4 in front of him as he crashed into the wall. The impact jarred loose a framed photo of a good-looking middle-aged couple with two teenage children, the same people he had avoided looking at two hours ago when they found the house. The frame shattered against the tiled floor and glass sprinkled the hallway.

He pushed off the wall almost at the same time as he caught a flicker of movement out of the corner of his right eye. It was coming from the patio window, which was in the process of sliding open—

Keo spun and fired—*pop-pop!*—and the window shattered, glass spraying everywhere. At the same time, a black-clad figure collapsed, followed by the clatter of a rifle falling against the wooden patio floor outside. He spent half a second wondering what the weapon was, and if the man had more ammo for it. That, and if it was the right caliber.

Not that he had time to check, because as soon as he fired his second shot, the door behind him *clicked* open. Keo felt the rush of wind and the August heat *(September heat? One of those.)* immediately flooding the first floor.

He turned, ready to fire, but there was no one on the other side of the hallway, just the open door and bright sunlight blasting him in the face—

A green oblong-shaped object appeared through the door and bounced across the floor.

Keo dived to his right, not even sure where that would take him, learning a heartbeat later that it was the kitchen. He landed painfully against the dust-covered floor and slid on his side across the room, slamming into the sink counter just as the explosion ripped apart the bottom of the stairs along with the table and cabinets in the dining room on the other side of the wall that separated it and the kitchen.

Smoke and debris flooded the entire floor.

Keo struggled back to his feet, sweeping the carbine right, then left. He made sure no one had tried to follow the dead man through the patio window in front of him before turning his attention back to the house's front door behind him.

The clatter of automatic gunfire echoed from upstairs. Norris, unloading on whoever was approaching the house from the north, out of the woods. Which meant there were at least three people assaulting them at the moment. He had killed one outside the patio, and another one had tossed the grenade. So how many was Norris shooting at? One more, at least, and two or three more if they were really unlucky.

Riiiiiight. Because we've been so lucky so far.

Keo scooted toward the hallway to his right connecting the front door, dining room, and the living room. He pressed his back against the smooth side of a silver refrigerator, which still managed to feel cool anyway despite going almost a year without electricity.

He listened, waiting for the sound of heavy footsteps that he knew was coming next. Besides the plentiful black assault vests and small arms, not to mention an ungodly amount of ammo, their pursuers also seemed to have a never-ending supply of army boots and other assorted military gear.

Who the hell are these guys?

But he didn't hear anything at the moment, which didn't make any sense.

What were they waiting for? Maybe they didn't think the grenade had taken him out, though more likely they were coordinating a plan of attack. If he had learned anything about these assholes, it was that they could be stubbornly patient. And why not? Sooner or later, there was going to be a lot more men in camo face paint gathering around the house. Retreating back to the house, as it turned out, hadn't been the best move on his and Norris's part.

"Norris!" Keo shouted. There hadn't been any shooting from upstairs in the last ten seconds, and silence from Norris was never a good sign.

After a few seconds, Norris shouted back down, "Yeah?"

"How's it looking up there?"

"I saw two!"

"You get 'em?"

"No! They're somewhere along the side of the house!"

"You need to shoot better!"

"Yeah, yeah. What about you?"

"Got one!"

"What was the big bang?"

"Grenade!"

"Damn!"

"Yeah."

Tactical gear. Assault rifles. Unlimited ammo. And now the enemy had grenades to throw around, too?

Who the hell are these guys?

Keo continued to wait. He had hoped the very loud back and forth with Norris would draw the grenade tosser forward, or at least prompt the man or one of his friends to make a move instead of just waiting for reinforcements. He needed to finish this before the others showed up.

"How many of you are out there?"

"A lot."

Doug wasn't lying, as it turned out.

Keo glanced quickly down at his watch: 3:16 P.M.

Late summer in Louisiana meant long days. Sunset didn't come until just before eight, which left them with four hours and thirty minutes (optimistically speaking) to survive this and find another place for shelter.

That took up most of his priorities these days—run, fight, evade, and shelter. When they could, they stayed at the same place for days, sometimes weeks, until they were forced to move on. He used to care about all the time they were wasting in the early days of the chase, which were usually filled with images of Gillian and his promise to her.

Not so much anymore. Now, finding a place that he and Norris could rest for more than one night in peace, without having to shoot at anyone—or be shot at—was as close to paradise as he could get. His standards for what qualified as a great day had fallen dramatically these last few months.

His watch ticked to 3:18 P.M.

Gotta get outta here.

Gotta get outta here soon…

CHAPTER 2

"YOU PROMISE ME," Gillian had said. *"You'll follow us to Santa Marie Island."*

"Yes," he had said. *"I promise."*

Even when he made it, he always knew there was a very good chance he wasn't going to be able to follow through. Not because he didn't want to, because God only knew he wanted to desperately. It was more that he didn't think he would get the chance. But he thought she needed to hear it at the moment, with heavily-armed men gathered all around them, trying to kill them.

The more things change…the more they don't.

He leaned around the corner of the kitchen and glanced back toward the front door for the fifth time in as many minutes. It was still wide open, sunlight pouring inside in big, comforting swaths. The foyer was in pieces, and so was the bottom of the stairs. Chunks of glass, what used to be fine mahogany wood, and a lot of someone's very expensive dinnerware set were scattered across the elongated open spaces.

We left our house for one weekend, and someone tosses a grenade inside. Man, this neighborhood's going to hell!

Keo felt like laughing at the absurd thought. The fact that he was making jokes made the absurdity even more so.

Keep laughing, pal. You're about to die, you know that, right?

He couldn't detect signs of movement or sounds of any kind. The house opened up to the shoreline, with the lake beyond about thirty meters or so connected to the front door by a winding cobblestone walkway walled by fields of unmowed grass. He remembered seeing a combination deck and empty boathouse there, including a pair of empty slots for jet skis. Like the boats, the jet skis were missing.

Who took all the boats? Maybe the same people that cleaned out all the houses before we got here. Curiouser and curiouser...

"Hey, kid!" Norris called from upstairs.

"Yeah!" Keo shouted back.

"You still alive?"

"I just said 'yeah,' didn't I?"

"Good point." There was a slight pause, then, "Can you make it?"

"Make it where?"

"Outside."

"I don't see how that's possible. You said there were two coming, and I definitely know there's one outside the front door right now."

"Well, we gotta make our move sooner or later. You know that, right?"

One hour. Maybe two, at the most.

Yeah, he knew it, all right.

"I'm open to suggestions," Keo said.

"I'm thinking—" Norris began, when Keo saw a black-gloved hand appear in the open doorway and toss a can-shaped object into the house.

"Incoming!" Keo shouted, and dived back behind the kitchen wall.

Something metallic clattered into the hallway and rolled along the tiled floor. There was a loud *pop!*, followed by the *swoosh!* of a smoke canister ripping.

"Smoke!" he shouted, hoping Norris could hear him over the sharp *hiss*.

He grabbed his T-shirt and pulled it up and over his mouth and nostrils—not that he expected it to do much good once the smoke reached him. He was still tugging at the fabric when he caught movement in front of him, outside on the patio.

Two figures, both clad in black, their faces smeared with green and black paint, were moving cautiously toward the broken window with weapons raised. They looked inside, searching for him in the kitchen. They spotted him as soon as he leaned out from behind the island counter to get a better look at them. Gunfire exploded and bullets tore into the wooden structure in front of him, chunks of the granite countertop splitting off like missiles. More bullets ricocheted off the steel refrigerator behind him, the *ping-ping-ping!* filling the first floor.

Keo kept his head down and bided his time, listening, listening—

Through the chaos, he heard the loud *thumping* footsteps he had been waiting for to finally show up, coming from behind him as their owner shuffled his way up the hallway from the front door.

When the two men finally emptied their magazines and stopped shooting, Keo held the M4 over what was left of the countertop and fired off a burst in the direction of the patio window. He had no clue if he hit anything or if the men were already inside the house. The last he saw of them, they were still cautiously approaching the shattered window, so maybe he caught them while they were still outside.

There was only one way to find out, though.

He stopped firing, pulled the rifle back, and dived forward, slipping and sliding against the dirt-covered but still slick floor. He braced himself for more return gunfire but was surprised when there was no reaction to his movements.

By now, smoke had filled half of the living room and pretty much the entire foyer, so when Keo picked himself up and ran, legs struggling for purchase against the wood and granite-covered floor, into the hallway, he didn't look up in time to see the figure coming straight at him. They collided, the impact sending the M4 flying out of his hands. The carbine hit the wall, the loud clatter unmistakable even as both he and the attacker went spilling to the floor.

Keo stabbed his hand down toward his hip, groping for the Glock G41 in its holster. The smoke stung his eyes, but he could just barely make out the form in front of him, a black shape scrambling up from the floor just a little slower than him. Unlike Keo, the man had managed to hold onto his weapon, an MP5K, despite the collision. His radio, on the other hand, hadn't survived the fall and pieces of it dangled from a Velcro strap along the left side of his vest. The man was whirling around in search of Keo, their entire world having been reduced to nothing but a thick white cloud and vision that was limited by only a few feet at a time.

The man finally located Keo, and as he lifted his weapon,

Keo shot him in the shoulder. He was aiming for the head, but the figure in front of him was moving too erratically, still spinning around, and it was a miracle he hit anything at all. A scream, then the body fell, the submachine gun falling away as the man grabbed at his wound.

Keo felt a burst of glee. The MP5K fired 9mm rounds, and its magazine was interchangeable with his now-depleted MP5SD. If the guy had spares, then that would mean more ammo for his weapon.

Daebak. Today's looking up!

The thought hadn't finished reverberating in his head when the loud pounding of footsteps coming from the living room snapped him back to reality.

The two from the patio.

The wounded black-clad man was trying to get back up when Keo slid behind him and hooked his left hand around the man's throat, pinning the back of his head to his chest, and shoved the barrel of the Glock against a trembling temple.

"Don't come any closer or your friend's dead!" Keo shouted into the white smoke.

The footsteps stopped.

Keo tightened his grip on the man's throat and leaned forward. "Tell them."

"Don't come any closer!" the man shouted.

Wait, what? That wasn't a man's voice—

Keo jerked the head back slightly and looked down at a woman's face. Bright blue eyes, made somehow brighter against the camo paint, peered defiantly back up at him. Late twenties, maybe early thirties—it was hard to tell with all the gunk on her face—and she had black hair in a ponytail.

"Fiona?" a male voice shouted from somewhere in the living room.

"I'm sorry!" the woman in front of Keo shouted back.

"Come any closer and her brain gets splattered on the walls!" Keo shouted.

He heard loud, grumbling curses, something that sounded like a brief argument, before the heavy footsteps echoed again—except this time they were fading, retreating back into the living room.

Jesus, I can't believe that worked.

He reached down and pulled a handgun out of the woman's hip holster and shoved it behind his waist. Then he grabbed her by the arm and pulled her up with him. She let out a scream.

"Sorry about that," Keo said, switching his grip from her injured left arm and over to her right.

"Go fuck yourself," she snarled back at him.

NORRIS CLEANED, DISINFECTED, and then bundled up the woman's shoulder using the first aid kit from his pack. It wasn't much of a wound—barely a graze, really—compared to what he had been carrying around through the woods of Louisiana for the last few months. Not that the woman seemed to appreciate her good fortune, or Norris's efforts to wrap her up.

He was back on the second-floor living room, with the stairs between him and Norris, finishing up with the woman on the opposite wall. The window was to his left, the stairs to his right. Keo had briefly considered retreating all the way into the bedrooms, but he didn't like the idea of being trapped in there.

Out here, if they could hold the stairs, they had some options left. Not a lot of good ones by any means, but some shitty options were better than none.

He glanced down at his watch. 3:54 P.M.

Still plenty of time…

They had been waiting for her friends to attack for the last thirty minutes, but the three men moving around somewhere below them hadn't shown any willingness to come up the stairs. Every now and then Keo expected them to just toss another grenade up here and kill them all, but that would have taken out Fiona, too, and they had already shown an unwillingness to harm her. So that was something he hadn't expected from their pursuers. Loyalty.

Fiona's eyes were locked on Keo, as if she thought she could kill him if she stared long and hard enough. He was almost tempted to hand her a gun and tell her to try it, but at the moment she was the only reason they were still alive.

"Give it a rest," Keo said.

"Which part of 'go fuck yourself' didn't you understand?" she said.

Norris chuckled. "Hey, look, she's just like you, kid. A hard-ass."

The ex-cop finished up and stuffed the first aid kit back into his pack before heading over to the bullet-riddled window and peeping outside from a safe angle. They didn't know if the sniper was still out there or not, or if the man had joined his buddies downstairs.

Keo stared back at Fiona. She sat with her legs splayed in front of her, hands on her lap, gauze tape covering the upper part of her left shoulder. Her assault vest lay on the floor nearby, with the broken radio still dangling from it. The black clothes she wore didn't do her any favors against the stifling heat, and neither did the camo that covered her face. Even with all that mess, he thought she was still reasonably attractive. Too bad she had been trying to kill him all day…

"You're dead," Fiona said, as if reading his mind. "Both of you. You know that, don't you? Neither one of you is getting out of this house alive."

"They'll have to come up and get us first," Keo said. "Apparently they care enough about you not to try it yet."

"You think you've figured it out?" There was just the ghost of a smile on her face. "You haven't figured out anything, dead man."

"Since I'm already a dead man, then you won't mind telling me who the fuck you people are."

"Now what would be the fun in that?"

"How many of you are out there?"

"More than enough to kill two assholes."

"So we're the assholes?" Norris said. "That's news to me."

"Did you think you were the good guys?" she said, almost laughing at him.

"You're the ones hunting us, lady," Keo said.

"You have no idea, do you?" she said.

"Enlighten us."

"Bobby."

Bobby?

The name sounded familiar, but he couldn't quite place it. "I don't know what you're talking about. I don't know any Bobby."

"Bullshit," Fiona said. "You started this when you killed

him."

"I told you. I don't know any Bobby. And I certainly never killed any Bobby. I would remember."

"You remember everyone you've killed?" she snorted.

"Yes," Keo said.

She stared at him in silence for a moment. Then, "How many people have you killed?"

You don't want to know, lady, he was going to say, but Norris interrupted him with, "That kid. Remember?"

Keo glanced at him. "What kid?"

"Back at the house. In the garage with Lotte? And Levy?"

Bobby.

Jesus Christ. The kid in the garage with Lotte. The one Levy killed?

"So now you remember him?" Fiona said. "Killing him started this. *You* started this."

"We didn't kill Bobby," Keo said. It wasn't a total lie, though the truth was more complicated.

"You did, someone else did, doesn't matter," Fiona said. "One of your people murdered Bobby. There were two others with him, but the way we heard it, that was a fair fight. Hell, for all I know, you killed Carl and Doug, too. That's five bodies on your doorsteps."

Carl and Doug?

He knew a Doug. Keo had shot a man who called himself Doug months ago when they had encountered him, along with a second man at an abandoned strip mall outside of Corden. Norris had shot the other one (*Carl, I presume*).

"Did you?" she asked.

"Did I what?" Keo said.

"Kill Carl and Doug, too?" She was watching him closely,

trying to read his reaction. "We never found their bodies, so we were never sure what happened to them…"

"I don't know who Carl and Doug are," Keo lied. "What makes you think we're the only people running around with guns out there? You seemed to have plenty of them yourself. What are you, ex-soldiers?"

"Nice try, but it's not going to be that easy."

"You don't look ex-military. Probably a wannabe."

"So that's your point of attack? Insult me and hope I'll blurt out something valuable when I indignantly try to defend myself?" She smirked then looked at Norris. "Is this guy calling the shots? If so, you're screwed, old man."

Norris grunted. "I've been telling myself that for the last nine months, girly. It's nothing I don't already know, so you can save your breath."

Keo looked down at his watch. "I don't have to survive your friends downstairs. I just have to outlast them until nightfall. I'm willing to bet those bedroom doors with a little furniture reinforcement will last a lot longer against the bloodsuckers than what your pals have to work with. What do you think?"

Her face was placid, almost…pitying? "You think the bloodsuckers are your biggest worry? They're not. It's not even me or my friends down there that you have to worry about. When you killed Bobby, you started something that can't be stopped. There's a man out there, and he's going to hunt you down to the ends of the Earth."

"'Hunt you down to the ends of the Earth'?" Keo said. "Jesus fucking Christ. Who the hell are you people?"

For a moment, he thought she was going to laugh, or maybe

mock him. But instead, she just shook her head. "You'll find out soon enough, because I'm one hundred percent certain he's on his way here now."

"Who?" Norris said. "*Who* is on his way here?"

She glanced back at Norris, then across the room at Keo. "You really don't know why any of this is happening, do you?"

"Not a goddamn clue, girly," Norris said.

"Well, that makes it kind of fucking tragic, doesn't it?" She sighed. "His name is Pollard. Bobby was his nephew."

"This is all because he blames us for killing Bobby?" Keo said. "Good old-fashioned revenge, is that it?"

"Not because of Bobby. Pollard liked the kid, but he didn't like him *that* much."

"What, then?"

"There was another boy with Bobby the day you killed—"

"We didn't kill him," Keo interrupted.

She shrugged indifferently. "The day he died, then. Better?"

"It's the truth," Norris said. "That used to count for something."

"Yeah, well, those days are long gone."

Norris grunted. "Tell me about it."

"If it matters to you, I believe you," she said.

"Why?" Keo said.

"Why?"

"Why do you believe that we didn't kill Bobby?"

"I don't have a clue," Fiona said. "But it doesn't seem like you'd have a reason to lie now. I mean, it's not like it's going to matter when Pollard gets here. He's still going to kill you because he blames you for it."

"But it's not for Bobby's death?" Norris said.

"No. That kid's death led to something else that matters more to Pollard than life itself. When Bobby died, there was another boy with him. Do you remember?"

*That sonofa*bitch.

Keo knew the name before she even said it. Somehow, he always knew the little bastard was going to keep haunting him for whatever little time he had left. All because he made the wrong decision in a moment of weakness, and for all the wrong reasons. It had been for Gillian, for the others, even Norris. He wanted to reward their faith in him. The world had ended, and he wanted desperately to be something new, someone other than what he had always embraced in the ten years prior.

"Joe," Fiona said. "The kid's name was Joe. Pollard, the man leading this hunt for you, is his father."

CHAPTER 3

FUCKING JOE.

He had no one to blame but himself. The Keo from October of last year would have put a bullet through the kid's head without wasting a second thinking about how it would make him feel later. But that was before he met Norris, Gillian, and the others. That was before the world ended.

Goddamn you, Joe, you little twerp.

Norris was probably thinking the same thing as he looked across the room at him, though there was something else in Norris's eyes, a *"Don't beat yourself up over it, kid"* that the ex-cop often gave him from time to time. Of course, Keo could just be seeing what he wanted to see at the moment, a pitiful attempt to lessen his own guilt.

I got soft. Jesus, when did I get so soft?

He returned his gaze to Fiona. She was watching him back with an almost curious expression. He imagined that she had been hunting him and Norris for so long she might have expected him to grow fangs and try to bleed her dry when they finally met. The enemy was always easier to put down when you saw them as less than human. He knew that personally. Maybe she had even convinced herself that he was like the creatures that came out at night.

That thought prompted him to look down at his watch again: 4:31 P.M.

Getting close…

"What now?" Fiona said.

Keo unzipped his pack and pulled out a sweat-soaked handkerchief that he tossed over to her.

She caught it with her good hand. "What am I supposed to do with this?"

"You really want to sit there all day with crap on your face?"

"Thanks, I guess."

Norris took out a bottle of water and tossed it over to her. She wet the rag and cleaned off the black and green paint. She wasn't bad looking, but Fiona was no Gillian. Then again, few people were even before the world ended, and there were even less of them now.

When she was done, Fiona turned the handkerchief over and cleaned the grime off her neck and wiped some of the blood off her left arm, careful not to touch the dressing. Then she drank the rest of the water.

"You're not what I expected," she said, looking across at him.

"What did you expect?"

"I don't know. Something else."

"Horns?"

"Maybe. I don't know."

"Sorry to disappoint."

"Yeah, well, I'm used to disappointments. It keeps you sane these days." She put the empty bottle between her legs and stared at her reflection in the plastic surface. "I wasn't lying to you when I said you're both dead men. Pollard isn't going to let you go, no matter how far you run. You killed his nephew and his son. He's never going to forgive that."

"Bobby was a mistake," Keo said. "We didn't kill him, but someone from our party did. Joe…he came after us. If he hadn't attacked the house—"

"It doesn't matter," she said, cutting him off. "The fact remains, his son is dead, and you were responsible."

"A man who loves his son wouldn't have given him face paint and an assault rifle and sent him out there to kill women and children," Norris said from the window. "The guy's idea of parental involvement stinks to high heaven."

"That may be," Fiona said. "Still doesn't change what happened. Or his response. This is what he wanted all along, you know. To corner you. When he puts his mind to something, Pollard is scary in the way he zeroes in."

"When I first saw them, Joe and the others didn't look paramilitary," Keo said. "They looked like regular hunters."

"They were scouting the area. It's better to look like hunters just strolling through the woods if you run across other survivors." She gave him a half-smile. "You'd be surprised how people react when guys with tactical assault gear roll up on them."

"No shit. You've done it before."

"Lots of times." She shrugged. "It's a dangerous world out there."

"Yeah, I guess it is," Keo said.

"What was this Pollard guy, ex-military?" Norris asked.

"I don't know," Fiona said. "I don't think anyone knows.

But some of the guys said he used to be an officer in the army."

"Why doesn't anyone know?" Keo asked.

"He won't say. Maybe you can ask him when you see him."

"I'll do that."

"Put a bullet in his head while you're at it, kid," Norris said.

"I'll make sure to do that, too."

"You mean that, don't you?" Fiona said. "You really think you're going to survive this, even get a chance to kill Pollard."

"I've survived worse."

"Have you?"

"Don't ask," Norris said. "This guy's past is murkier than the mud your boys have been forcing us to traipse through the last three months."

"Two and a half," Keo said.

"You sure?"

"Pretty sure."

Probably.

"What did you do before all of this?" she asked Keo.

"I worked for some guys based out of Raleigh, North Carolina."

"He used to be a mercenary," Norris said.

"Eh, we've been called various things," Keo said. "Some more unseemly than others. Mercenaries is just one."

"What are the other things people have called you?" Fiona asked.

"Why the curiosity?"

"Just curious."

He smiled. "A lot of other things, depending on what we do. But mostly, we stay in the shadows."

"Why?"

"Hard to shoot something you can't see." He added, "It's a living. Well, it was a living."

"Sounds like a dangerous way to make a living."

He gave her a noncommittal shrug.

She waited for him to continue, and when he didn't, she said, "What kind of name is Keo, anyway?"

"Bill was taken," Keo said.

"HOW MANY?" KEO asked.

"Too many," Norris said.

Keo leaned against the wall and peered out the bullet-riddled window across from Norris. Humid air flowed through the holes and merged with the already stale interior of the house's second floor. He ignored the heat and concentrated on the figures moving across the ground, darting between a field of trees and toward them.

He counted six. Add that to the two already below them (or was it three?), and it was eight people at least. All of them armed with assault rifles and, as far as he knew, an unlimited supply of ammo and God knew what else they had in their arsenal. Fiona had, after all, tried to take him out with a grenade and a smoke canister. What did the ones waiting below them have? Or the six coming over?

Screwed doesn't even begin to describe this lovely day.

He thought about taking a shot at the closest black-clad figure moving between the trees. The man was doing his best to stay hidden, even employing a zig-zag pattern as he raced out from behind cover.

Keo decided against it. He needed to conserve ammo right now. He counted a magazine and a half for the M4, which was now his backup weapon. The loaded magazine only had ten bullets left, while he had a full spare in one of his pouches. There were also the two reloads for the Glock, which still had almost a full mag ready to go. But handguns weren't going to do much against eight *(at least)* people with assault rifles. The upside was that Fiona had attacked him with a Heckler & Koch MP5K. She had also been carrying three spares for her submachine gun with thirty rounds each, which meant he now had three spares for his MP5SD since the two weapons utilized compatible steel magazines. That, more than anything, was the best damn news he had gotten all day.

"More will come," Fiona said behind them.

Keo glanced back at her. He was surprised she hadn't decided to risk running for the stairs while his back was turned. The distance was less than eight meters and she could probably have made it if she got a good enough jump. He pegged her chances at fifty-fifty, which wasn't bad. Hell, he would have gone for it.

So I guess she's smarter than me.

"How many more?" Keo asked.

"It depends on how close Pollard is. How many did you see out there?"

Keo glanced over at Norris, who shrugged.

"Six," Keo said.

"Then Pollard isn't here yet. When he comes, you'll know it."

"How many is he bringing?" Norris asked.

"It could be anywhere from ten to twenty, depending on

who else is nearby. He has most of them stationed at the visitors' building near the entrance of the park."

"How many there?" Keo asked.

"Maybe twenty more? The rest were in the woods, pushing you guys down here. You didn't think you ended up pinned against the south shoreline by accident, did you? This was Pollard's plan all along."

"How many people does he have out there?" Norris asked. He sounded slightly exasperated by all the numbers Fiona was throwing at them.

"Fifty, give or take," Fiona said. "Not counting the ones you've killed already. There are more back in Corden." She frowned. "I told you. It doesn't matter where you go. Pollard will follow you all the way to hell, and he's got people who will do everything he tells them."

Keo and Norris exchanged another look. He was pretty sure he had just seen something that looked more than a little bit like fear in the ex-cop's eyes that time. He wondered what Norris was seeing in his.

Fifty more. That was how many men Pollard had with him at the moment. Not counting the ones already below, or the ones that just showed up. Just short of sixty. Maybe over sixty.

Fucking Joe.

He looked back at Fiona. "What about you?"

"What about me?" she said.

"What will Pollard do when he gets here?"

She shook her head. He could tell that she had been think-ing about the same question all this time, and she didn't look as if she liked her own conclusions. "If you're asking me will Pollard do everything in his power to make sure I don't die along with you two, then you're barking up the wrong tree. He doesn't give a shit about me. I'm expendable. We all are to him."

"Those two down there backed away when I had you at gunpoint. They seemed to give plenty of shits about you."

She nodded. "Eric and Wally are my friends. I would do the same for them."

"But Pollard…"

"He's not my friend." She stared at him stone-faced. "Once he shows up, he's going to send in people who don't care if I live or die. Their primary goal will be to take the two of you."

"Why would he do that?" Norris asked.

"What do you mean?"

"What he means is, you had a grenade," Keo said. "You were trying to kill us. Why would Pollard throw men up here to capture us now?"

"It's his MO. Pollard was willing to just kill you when you were out there running around. But now that you're cornered, he'll want more. He'll demand his pound of flesh. He'll want to take his time with the two of you because he can afford to now."

"Damn," Norris said. "This guy sounds like a ball of laughs. How'd you get involved with a charmer like that, kid?"

"It's the end of the world, old man," Fiona said, as if that should explain it.

Keo guessed that it did.

You survive. Even if that means following someone like Pollard. Because doing so means you get to keep surviving…

"You killed Pollard's only son," Fiona said, leaning her head back against the wall. "He loved that boy. Doted on him. The only reason he let Joe attack the house was because he thought he had it all planned out, and his second-in-command was leading the charge."

"He down there now?" Norris asked. "This second-in-command?"

"That'd be a hell of a feat. Pollard tied him to a tree and left him outside at night after he came back without Joe. We could hear him screaming throughout the night. I swear, they were messing with him, taking their time."

"What do you mean?" Keo said. "Who was messing with him?"

"The creatures," Fiona said. "The bloodsuckers. I'd never seen anyone take that long to die. He must have screamed until almost sunrise…"

5:05 P.M.

Running out of time…

He could hear them moving below on the first floor, sometimes racing past the stair landing or going back and forth around the house on the outside. Every now and then, there was the distant squawk of a radio call, but they were either too far away or too hidden behind walls for him to make out what they were saying. One thing was for sure: they weren't going to attack. At least, not yet.

They're waiting for Pollard…

"Where was he when you last saw him?" Keo asked Fiona. "Pollard."

"At the visitors' building," she said. "He doesn't do the

dirty work. Running around after you two is for grunts like me."

"Sounds like a swell guy," Norris said.

"He's an officer," Keo said. "That's what they do. Give orders, then wait for someone else to make it happen."

"I thought you weren't ex-military," Fiona said.

"I wasn't. But I've been around enough of them."

"Your dad was one, right?" Norris said.

"An officer? No. He was a working man. It was one of his better qualities, and he didn't have very many to begin with."

"Daddy issues, huh?" Fiona said.

"Not really," Keo said. "He's dead and I'm still alive."

"Definitely daddy issues."

"I'm not the one following a maniac through half of Louisiana."

"Point taken," she sighed.

He got up and moved toward the stairs and leaned around the newel, then took a quick glance down at the first floor. From up here, he could see straight down to the damaged bottom half. Fiona's grenade had gutted almost one third of the steps, leaving behind just enough for him to lead her up at gunpoint earlier. That was another accidental plus. It made the path unnecessarily treacherous for those downstairs, especially if there were more than one coming up at the same time.

"Anything?" Norris said behind him.

"Not a peep."

"They're going to wait you out until Pollard shows up," Fiona said. "It's funny..."

"What's that?" Keo said.

"Everyone liked Bobby, Pollard's nephew. He was a good kid. But Joe? No one really liked the little bastard. He was always too aware of his position. Or his father's, anyway. He always knew what buttons to push to get things his way. Sweet and innocent one moment, then a real smarmy asshole the next."

And he was a hell of an actor, too.

Norris was looking at him curiously. "What're you thinking, kid?"

"When Pollard shows up, it's over."

"Yeah, I figured that part out by my little lonesome. So what are we gonna do about it, that's the question."

Keo grinned. "What would Riggs do in this situation?"

Norris laughed. "I think you know the answer to that one."

"Who's Riggs?" Fiona asked.

Keo got up and walked back to the wall where he had placed Fiona's pack. He rifled through the contents and pulled it out. It sported camouflage colors and was slightly five inches long and one-and-a-half inches wide, with a pin at one end.

He looked over at Norris. "You ready for this, old-timer?"

"No," Norris said, "but when has that ever stopped your crazy ass from doing something anyway?"

"Um, what's going on, guys?" Fiona said, more than just a touch of worry in her voice.

"Have you ever seen *Lethal Weapon?*" Keo asked her.

"What is that, a movie?"

"Yeah. Apparently it was a big action series from the '80s."

"And '90s," Norris added.

"Right, and '90s."

"So?" Fiona said. "What's that got to do with what you're about to do now?"

Norris chuckled. "You gotta grow the mullet, kid."

"If I survive this, I'll think about it," Keo said.

CHAPTER 4

THE SMOKE WOULD last for ninety seconds. It was a thick, billowing white cloud that engulfed the bottom of the stairs almost as soon as it touched down. The speed with which it spread was impressive, though Keo wished Fiona had been carrying a third canister with her. Two of these bad boys would have been ideal.

He went down first with the MP5SD, fully intending to rely on its sound suppressor capability as he moved through the makeshift camouflage. He didn't have any illusions that whatever advantage he had purchased was going to last for very long. There were eight people down there—*at least*—and they were all heavily armed. His only hope was that they had become complacent since arriving, knowing nothing was going to happen until Pollard arrived.

The first man he saw was coughing, swiping his hand in the air and stumbling around near the stair landing. His black clothes made him easy to spot against the white smoke. He had come from the direction of the kitchen, his AK-47 pointing at the floor in front of him. Keo wondered where he was going. For half a second, anyway.

The submachine gun went *pfft-pfft!* in Keo's hands as he shot the man once in the chest, then again as the body fell to the floor in front of him.

Norris was coming down behind him, the bigger man moving with difficulty down the destroyed bottom half of the stairs. Keo kept to the side, skirting around the damaged area, then hopped the last four steps. Unlike last time when he stumbled and crashed into the wall, this time he landed in a slight crouch next to the dead body lying facedown on its stomach.

Voices, screaming, and radios squawking exploded all around him.

"The house!" someone shouted. "They're coming down! Converge converge converge now!"

Now there's a man with his head on straight.

Keo straightened up and twisted right, toward the living room. He hadn't even completed his turn yet when he caught a ripple of movement in the expanding smoke. He fired twice and hit something that sounded like glass as the figure disappeared out of his line of sight.

More footsteps. Coughing. *From behind him.*

He spun all the way around, just as a large black-clad silhouette staggered through the open door. Keo knew the front door was wide open because he could see the rectangular opening, like some kind of extra-dimensional portal with the sun glowing brightly on the other side. That, and the cloud was flooding in that direction, being sucked out by the hot air.

Keo shot the man once and hit him in the neck. Then as the man stumbled into a wall, gagging, blood spurting out of the hole just under his chin, Keo put a second round into his chest. The man slid down the wall with a heavy *thump*, his rifle clattering beside him.

There was loud, crashing gunfire behind him as Norris unleashed at the other side of the house with his M4. Norris was standing too close when he fired, and Keo flinched at the thunderous booms, one after another after another.

"Go, kid, go!" Norris shouted.

Keo made a run for the door. He hopped over chunks of the wall, ceiling, and floor that had been gutted by Fiona's grenade from earlier. Loose tiles *crunched* under him, but the sound was quickly lost in another volley of bullets as Norris sprayed into the living room again. Keo just hoped the ex-cop was keeping count of his magazine, because he wasn't entirely sure if they were going to have a chance to reload before this was over.

How long had it been? The smoke wasn't going to last for more than ninety seconds.

Was it thirty seconds yet? Maybe a minute?

He was losing track of time. It probably had something to do with the hammering in his chest. He did his best to not breathe in the smoke as he ran through it, wishing the damn foyer wasn't so long and—

Another black figure appeared in the doorway, the radio Velcroed to his assault vest blaring with someone's voice, shouting, "They're making a run for the door! Who the hell is at the door?"

This guy, Keo thought, and shot the man in the face from almost point-blank range.

Blood and brains might have exited the back of the man's head and sprayed the suffocating hot summer air behind him, but it was difficult to see through the smoke and bright sun assaulting every one of his senses.

Then he was through, jumping over the falling body even before the assaulter had gone completely down.

"Norris!" he shouted.

"Behind you!" Norris shouted back. "Keep moving!"

Keo kept moving, bursting out into the opening and landing on the cobblestone pathway that connected the door, snaked around the front yard, and reached the boathouse on Downey Creek Lake. It was a damn shame there wasn't a boat in there waiting for them.

Where the hell are all the boats?

Considering how much lead Norris was pouring into the house behind him, Keo guessed most of the assaulters were back there. He had killed three—one was coming out of the kitchen, but two were clearly guarding the front door—so that left five out back. Unless he had hit the fourth man he saw moving earlier, then maybe four. Not that one more or less made any bit of difference at the moment.

Keo didn't go down the pathway for very long. After about a second, he turned right and darted through overgrown grass that went up almost to his knees. It was like running across quicksand, only with more things slapping at his legs as he went.

The house was to his right, the thick woods spread out on all sides except to his left where the lake was. One of the reasons they had chosen the house was because of its isolated location. It was far from the other homes and connected to the main road by a private driveway. The problem with that was there wasn't another house for them to run to for cover, and once outside the front door they were essentially out in the open, with the tree line (their only option) nearly forty meters away across open field.

No sweat. Time to run for your life, pal.

Keo ran, the MP5SD clutched tightly in his hands, ready to shoot anything that popped up in front of him. Sweat poured down his temple and stung his eyes, and it had only been a few seconds since he came out of the house.

Goddamn, it was hot out here.

It took five (or was that ten?) seconds before the first gunshot *zipped!* past his head, so close he swore the damn thing might have singed a stray hair or two as it went. After that first shot, the bullets started coming faster, like bees *buzzing* around him. Bees made of lead. One bite and he was a goner. He already had two holes in him; a third might just about do it. Especially in the right place—

"Too many!" Norris shouted behind him.

Keo threw a quick glance back and saw Norris struggling to keep up. The older man was already sucking in air like a drowning victim, the M4 swinging wildly in front of him. Keo had never seen him look more tired or ready to drop. And they had only been running for...what was it now, twenty seconds...? Ten? *Five seconds?*

He looked past Norris at two figures emerging out of the front door of the two-story house further back, the white smoke billowing out with them, turning them into specters instead of assholes with assault rifles. Two more were coming from around the side of the house, both running full speed and firing in their direction at the same time.

"Keep running!" Keo shouted.

"No, no," Norris said. "We gotta split up!"

"Are you crazy?"

Norris grinned at him. It was a slightly unhinged look, and Keo wondered if *he* ever looked like that whenever Norris called him crazy and he grinned back at the ex-cop in response.

"We stick together!" Keo shouted.

"Okay, okay, just keep going!" Norris shouted back.

Keo faced forward again. The wall of trees was coming up.

Ten meters.

Five...

Tree barks shattered in front of him from stray bullets. Well, not stray, exactly. Those bullets definitely had a target. Him and Norris.

Then he was through!

He breathed a sigh of relief, though he didn't stop running for even a nanosecond. Soft and slightly damp earth squelched under his shoes instead of the hard, sun-drenched ground of the house front yard. The cool relief from the shade provided by the dome of trees was immediately obvious. And it was only going to get cooler, because soon it would be night, and night meant...

Run! Stop thinking and run!

"We keep going until we hit the shoreline!" Keo shouted. "Then follow it back around to the west side of the park!"

He waited for Norris to respond.

"Norris!"

Keo risked slowing down a bit. Not a lot, just enough to be able to glance over his shoulder—where he saw nothing back there.

He slid to a stop and grabbed at the gnarled face of a tree and used the moment to catch his breath while he looked around for Norris. There were no signs of him.

Where the hell did Norris go, and how long had he been running all by himself?

"Norris!"

He realized what a stupid thing that was to do immediately and almost paid for it with his life when a black-clad figure thirty meters away, barely visible behind some trees, turned in his direction and snapped off a shot.

The tree he had been holding onto sent splintered bark in his face. Keo cursed and squeezed off three shots back in the man's direction. He couldn't really see who he was shooting at because his eyes were half closed. It felt like needles had been hammered into his eyeballs. He did see a black blob ducking for cover, and Keo used the opportunity to spin around and take off running again.

He waited for the man to unload on him, but maybe the guy didn't have a shot, or maybe Keo was a lot faster than he ever gave himself credit for. Either way, he kept moving, not looking back, doing his best to blink away whatever was trying to drill their way into his eyes and the brain behind them.

At least he wasn't blind. He knew that much, because he could see the trees coming up at him from all sides. Left, right, and front. Everywhere. Every tree looked identical to the last one hundred he had already passed.

He had been running for ten (*fifteen?*) seconds when he heard gunfire from behind him. He braced himself for a new swarm of bees, but they never came. That was because the shooting wasn't anywhere nearby.

It was coming from behind and to the right of him.

Norris.

He stopped for a moment, slipping behind a big tree for

cover, and looked back with the MP5SD at the ready. The rattle of automatic gunfire continued, like rolling thunder smashing across Robertson Park, and they were moving *away* from him.

What the hell are you doing, Norris?

Then, just like that, the last shot faded and there was just...silence.

He waited and waited for more shooting, but there was none. There was just the quiet all around him. He didn't know silence could be so utterly suffocating.

Norris...

He was either dead, or he had escaped his pursuers. The only way to know for sure would be to head back to the house and pick up Norris's trail and locate him...or his body. It was a hell of a choice. If Norris had managed to get away, then Keo would be heading right back into the teeth of the bad guys—

The squawk of a radio from nearby and the sound of a male voice intruded on his thoughts. "Did you get them? Someone answer me."

Keo didn't recognize the slightly muffled voice, but he knew a man in a position of authority when he heard one, even through a radio's tiny speakers. His life was spent taking orders from men who knew the value of their words, and the man he was listening to now understood that power and wielded it without hesitation.

"We're looking for them now, sir," a voice on the other side of the tree he was positioned behind answered. The man wasn't *too* close because Keo had to strain a bit to hear all the words clearly. "I think they split up."

There was a moment of silence before the second man answered through the radio. "Find them quick. You're running out of time."

"Yes, sir."

Keo stood perfectly still and listened to the man with the radio walking past him. When he was sure the footsteps were fading, he slowly slipped around the tree to get a better look. A figure in black clothes and assault vest was picking his way through the woods cautiously when he suddenly picked up speed. A second later, he was jogging through the woods, heading north up the park, until he slipped through some underbrush and was gone.

He cursed under his breath. He could have used the man's radio. That, more than anything, would have allowed him to keep tabs on his pursuers.

Too late now. Way too late now.

Keo turned and continued west along the shoreline.

There was some good news. The man had said into the radio, *"We're looking for them now, sir."* That meant they hadn't captured Norris yet, so the old-timer was still out there somewhere.

Keo smiled. Sometimes he didn't give Norris enough credit. Of course, reuniting with the ex-cop might be a problem. But that was for another day.

He glanced upward. The woods were thick and the tree crowns were dense, but he could make out the sun. It was still high up, but it wasn't going to stay that way for very long.

His watch confirmed it: 5:24 P.M.

The man on the radio was right. Time was running out, a thought that made him walk with more urgency without even realizing it.

There were possible shelters all around him in the form of

the other houses. All he needed was one of them. The problem with that was Pollard's people could easily deduce that would be his goal (it wasn't rocket science, after all), which meant they could use their overwhelming force to check every house in the vicinity. If he picked the wrong one, they would start this little gunfight all over again, and this time he would be alone. He didn't like his chances of surviving that at all.

As he trudged on, keeping his ears open and still trying to blink out whatever the hell he had gotten in his eyes, Keo thought about what else Fiona had said about Pollard. She all but confirmed that she followed the ex-Army officer out of basic necessity. He didn't blame her one bit. He had spent most of his life looking out for himself, but these days you needed someone to watch your back. He'd been lucky all these months with Norris.

Not anymore.

He kept moving, and with each step, he expected to hear hints that Norris was still out there somewhere.

A gunshot. A scream. Voices. *Anything.*

The utter peace and tranquility of the park, for some reason, depressed and filled him with pessimistic thoughts.

CHAPTER 5

SO THIS IS what it's like to be a squirrel.

The thought flashed across his mind as he leaned back against the massive tree trunk and tried to balance himself on the large branch. It was the widest thing he had been able to find after thirty minutes of searching, keeping one eye on the dwindling sunlight around him at the same time.

Sunlight, sunlight, don't go away...

The coming darkness had always felt like a tightening noose even when he was with Gillian and the others at Earl's house. But now, running for his life through the woods, it was even more pronounced, the rope thicker and more unyielding. The overwhelming need to constantly look for shelter, even when it was still morning, had dominated every waking hour since he and Norris began fleeing Pollard's people.

Pollard's people.

It was a curious sensation to finally have a name to go with the black assault vests and painted faces. He used to just refer to them as *assaulters* in his head, but now he had a name and a history, even a voice if not a face. But that was coming. Keo didn't have any delusions that Pollard was going to give up the search now. Not when he was so close. The man had to know there were no places for Keo to go except north out of the park.

That was the point of pushing him and Norris down here in the first place. They had been herded like cattle all this time; they just hadn't known it.

Maybe I can build a boat. Or a canoe. Like on Gilligan's Island. *Where's the Professor when you need him? Hell, right now I'd settle for Mary Ann. Maybe use her as bait...*

His watch ticked to 7:22 P.M.

Not that he needed the confirmation. He was up high enough that he could see past most of the canopy and at the darkening skies beyond. He would have called it cloudy, except there hadn't been any rain in four to five days.

He tightened his grip on the MP5SD resting in his lap and watched the squirrel staring back at him from a much thinner branch across the open space. The animal looked intrigued by Keo's presence, perhaps wondering what a human was doing all the way up here in its domain. It sure didn't look scared of him. Then again, after what it had probably seen racing around down below, a regular ol' man probably didn't rate very high on its list of "things to fear."

Keo thought about shooting it. He hadn't had squirrel meat in months. The last time was when Levy shot a couple of the furry critters and brought them back to the house. They had made squirrel stew that night. The animal was surprisingly tasty, but then again, maybe it was just how Levy cooked it.

Levy.

When was the last time he actually thought about him in any detail? It had been a while, so long that he couldn't recall.

Levy was dead. Along with Lotte and Jill.

What about Gillian? And Jordan and Mark? Rachel and her daughter, Christine?

Are you still alive out there, Gillian? Are you still waiting for me, or have you given up?

He wished he knew if she had ever made it to Santa Marie Island. His one comforting thought was that Jordan was with her, and she was as competent a survivor, man or woman, as Keo had come across since the end of the world. She had single-handedly kept her friends Mark and Jill alive for months. The only person he would have trusted Gillian's life with more than Jordan was Norris, and Norris was…out there somewhere.

Maybe dead. Maybe alive.

Maybe. Too many maybes. That was the problem. That was always the problem. The uncertainty of it all. Where he was going, what he was doing, why he was doing it, and what the hell was happening out there in the rest of the world.

But he couldn't think of all that right now. He had to stay in the present. And right now, the present was precarious.

He glanced down reflexively at his watch again: 7:39 P.M.

Time flies when you're sitting in a tree, having a staring contest with a squirrel…

HE WAS THIRTY meters up from the ground, give or take a couple of meters. It hadn't been an easy climb, but then his mom always did call him *wonsungi* (or "monkey," as he later found out) for a reason. When you were an Army brat living on strange bases around the world, it helped to be able to entertain yourself. A tree was a lot easier to find and befriend.

Now, as Keo looked down at the horde of undead things moving below him, he wished he had climbed just a little bit higher. Maybe all the way to the top. Fifty meters. Maybe sixty would have been about just right. Or higher...

He stopped counting after the fiftieth creature glided under him and through the woods as if they didn't even need to touch the ground. Of course, that was impossible. The bloodsuckers may be light on their feet, thanks to their skeletal frames and non-existent muscle mass, but they hadn't mastered the ability of flight just yet.

At least, as far as he knew.

Who knew what they would be capable of in another year. Or ten years. Or a hundred. Could they even die? God knew they couldn't be killed. He had seen plenty of them still moving even without a head. How was that even *possible?*

Keo didn't remember when he had stopped breathing, but he wasn't aware of his chest rising and falling as he watched them flitting across the soft ground. If it was dark outside the park, it was nearly pitch-black inside, and all Keo could really make out were silhouetted, deformed monstrosities that shouldn't exist but did. The loud *crunch-crunch* of leaves and the *snap!* of twigs were like hundreds of tiny firecrackers going off all at once.

Bloodsuckers. Creatures. *Things* that shouldn't be alive, but were.

Where did they come from? Where were they hiding during the day? Some of them had to have been nesting inside the houses along the shoreline. How else could they have appeared so fast? The activity began almost as soon as night fell, the sound of their footsteps like stampeding animals getting louder as they got closer and their numbers swelled. At one point, he lost sight of the ground completely because there were so many of them, like a black ocean of tar swallowing up the world.

Should have kept climbing…all the way to the moon…

Mercifully, they were starting to thin out now, and he could finally see the dirt and trampled foliage again. There were still the occasional creatures racing across, trailing behind the others. He wondered if they had gotten lost somewhere. Or maybe they overslept. That made him smile despite himself.

Back when the woods were clogged with their unending numbers, he had been forced to pinch his nostrils against their smell. It was a pungent odor, undeniable and everywhere at once. Even breathing through his mouth became ineffective after a while.

Like rotting cabbage left out in the sun…then mixed with shit. Cat shit.

Climbing the tree instead of running to the closest house for shelter was a no-brainer, especially with everything he knew about Pollard. Not just what Fiona had told him, but what he had discovered about the man from his actions. There was no doubt in his mind that spending a night in any of the surrounding houses would have resulted in a gunfight or capture. So he did the unthinkable (some might even say *crazy*; Norris definitely would) and stayed inside the woods.

Or, well, above it. Mostly above it, anyway.

He liked to think he was smarter than a squirrel, and those creatures had figured out how to survive the nights. *Stay off the ground.* It was a simple enough concept, but one that he and Norris rarely embraced unless they absolutely had to, like the first night Pollard's people chased them into the woods—

Keo froze in place. He might have also ceased breathing again.

Two of them had appeared out of the shadows and stopped a dozen or so meters from the tree where he was perched, unmoving. They were standing so close to one another—or were they hunched over? It was hard to tell from this high up— that for a moment they almost looked like lovers holding hands during a walk in the moonlight. Which was absurd, and he realized that quickly when one lifted its head and sniffed the air.

Can it smell me?

Why couldn't they smell him, though? He could smell *them* just fine, even from a distance. Then again, he didn't reek like they did. Or at least, he hoped he didn't. When was the last time he took a shower? Or changed clothes?

Too long ago. Way too long ago.

Keo flicked the fire selector on the submachine gun to full-auto. It was an instinctive response, because he knew shooting them did nothing. It didn't even slow them down, for God's sake. But maybe if they started climbing he could knock them back down with a well-placed shot to the head. Or in the eyes. Could they still see without eyes? Oh, hell, of course they could. They could "see" without a *head*.

If all else failed, he could just smash their faces in with the stock—

One of the creatures took off, bounding out of his peripheral vision with surprising speed. The second one remained behind, still sniffing the air around it, as if it knew— somehow—that he was nearby, but was unable to locate him. Maybe that even frustrated it. Could they get frustrated? At times he had seen some of the creatures show something that looked like human emotions. Irritation, annoyance, and once, even fear.

Or was it all in his mind? Was he assigning them familiar human traits in an attempt to make them easier to understand? The mind did strange things when it was confronted with impossible realities. Maybe he was simply coping—

The creature raced off after the first one, the *crunch-crunch* of its footsteps fading into the darkening night.

Keo finally let himself breathe again.

Close one. That was a real close one there, pal.

He closed his eyes briefly. Not for long. Maybe a few seconds. Slowly, very slowly, he lowered his heart rate and only allowed himself to relax when he was taking normal breaths through his nostrils again.

He heard a scratching noise and looked up and across from him.

The furry thing stood on its hind legs, on the same branch it had appeared on this evening when it engaged him in a staring contest. It had disappeared when the bloodsuckers started showing up, leaving Keo to wonder where it went. Apparently it had been triumphant during its absence, because the animal now had an acorn squeezed between two small hands. It was definitely the same squirrel from earlier, he was sure of it.

Probably.

He watched it watching him back across the small distance. Somehow, even though the semidarkness, he could see the animal clear as day.

What was it thinking now? Maybe once again trying to figure out what a human was doing trying not to fall asleep on a tree branch that could snap under him at any second and send him plummeting back down to the ground, to the black-skinned and deformed things that ruled the night.

Or maybe it was just a dumb, furry thing chipping away at an acorn with its teeth.

I'm trying to understand the motivations of a squirrel while sitting on a tree branch and trying not to fall off and die a grisly death (or worse).

Does life get any better than this?

HE COULDN'T GO to sleep. He couldn't afford to. The branch was wide enough to sit on, but it wasn't going to catch him if he flopped over the side while dozing off. He couldn't allow that to happen, so Keo tried every trick in the book to stay awake.

It was easy the first few hours, but his eyelids started to get heavy around ten. He had to resort to all those years of experience, all those hours of sleepless nights when staying awake meant the difference between life and death, getting paid and…well, dead people didn't care about bank accounts anymore, did they?

He drank the remaining two bottles of water he had left in his pack. Dehydration caused fatigue, and fatigue caused drowsiness. He managed to space the liquid out until midnight when he finally tasted the last drop.

Around one, he began pulling on his earlobes and rubbing the back of his hands between his thumb and index finger to keep alert. When that lost its effect after about an hour, he lifted his legs and pressed against the back of his knees. After a while, he resorted to pinching different parts of his body.

When he started to become immune to those acupuncture tricks at around two in the morning, he did stretching exercises with his arms, reaching up, sideways, and twisting his torso in every direction possible. He couldn't do much with the limited space and the fragility of the branch under him, but they were enough to keep him active and stave off sleep for a little while longer.

He moved onto breathing exercises around four o'clock, sucking in air through his nose and pulling in his abdomen toward his diaphragm with every exhale. He did it just quickly enough to make the exercise effective while still not making too much noise.

Because he could still hear them down there. They weren't moving directly under him anymore, and they were more spread out now, but the woods were so quiet (even the birds knew better than to make too much noise up on their high perches) that it was easy to pick out their scratching movements from long distances.

It occurred to him a few hours ago that the creatures weren't running blind around the park. They were, in fact, surging in the same direction all throughout the night—northwest. There was a reason for that. Pollard's people were in that direction, gathered at the park visitors' building. Fiona had told him that, and the creatures always seemed to just know where people were hiding, especially in large clusters.

The cities. I wonder what the cities were like in the early days...?

His brief happiness that the monsters were potentially, right now, cutting into Pollard's numbers went out the window when he waited and waited and didn't hear a single gunshot. There should have been a lot of it, because there was no way in hell

Pollard's well-armed little paramilitary unit would go down without a fight. So what did the silence mean? Maybe the creatures did find Pollard's group but couldn't get to them. Pollard's men, in turn, might be too disciplined to shoot unnecessarily.

All the while, he was stuck up a tree, desperately trying not to fall asleep.

It was five in the morning when he glanced down at his watch for the tenth time in the last two hours.

That was the good news. Sunrise came early during the summers. All he had to do was stay awake for two more hours...

SHIT!

He snapped awake, reaching blindly out to grab at some-thing—*anything*—and just barely managed to wrap his fingers around a thick branch directly above him while his other hand was flailing wildly in open space. The MP5SD had fallen off his lap during his little almost-drop, but luckily the strap had kept it from dropping to the ground below; instead, it just dangled from his shoulder.

*Sonofa*bitch.

He righted himself, sucking in a deep breath.

He had almost died. Almost fallen right off the tree and died. Because there was no way he was going to make it back up if he fell. The noise alone would have brought at least a dozen *(hundreds)* of the bloodsuckers still *crunching* and *snapping* along the woods all around him. It was so quiet they would have easily heard a big dummy like him landing on the ground.

Close. Real close one there, pal.

He looked down at his watch again: 5:16 A.M.

Christ. It hadn't even been much of a nap. A few minutes, at the most. A few more seconds and—

He pulled the submachine gun up by the strap and placed it back in his lap, then stared off at nothing. For some reason, his mind wandered back to Fiona.

Was she back with Pollard now? Probably. There was no reason for her not to go back. Would he punish her for getting captured? Maybe. Ironically, the fact that Keo had shot her in the shoulder might have saved her life. It was hard to blame someone for getting snatched after they had taken a bullet while executing your orders. Hard, but not impossible. Given what Fiona had told him about Pollard and what had happened to the man's former second-in-command, the ex-officer apparently didn't take failure very well.

Screw you, Pollard. Your kid had it coming.

Thinking about Fiona made him feel slightly guilty for some reason, so he thought about Gillian instead. The last time he had seen her, her hair was almost down to her waist. And those deep green eyes. She was back at Santa Marie Island right now. Or, at least, he hoped she was. If not, then all of this would have been for nothing.

5:32 A.M.

Almost there…

HE CLIMBED DOWN with sunlight at his back. The warmth was as soothing now—maybe even more so—as all the other mornings. The growing heat around him was all the confirmation he needed to finally escape back down to solid ground.

He scooted down the length of the tree, surprised at his own speed and agility for someone who hadn't slept all night. It was probably the adrenaline and the exhilaration of still being alive after almost dying more than once in the last twenty-four hours.

Keo hopped the last few meters and landed in a crouch. He stood up and immediately unslung the MP5SD.

Crunch!

He spun around, lifting the submachine gun, but it wasn't halfway up when he saw the barrel of the rifle pointed straight at him and he stopped moving entirely. Another inch, and there would be a loud *boom!* and a hole would appear in the very center of his chest. Or head, if the guy was a really good shot, which at this distance, he didn't really have to be.

The man behind the camouflaged rifle was leaning behind a tree twenty meters from him. Too close to miss, even if he was covered from head to toe in...*what the hell?* It took Keo a few seconds to realize the man was wearing a ghillie suit put together from materials abundant in the park, namely leaves, mud, and grass.

Keo was frozen in place. It would only take a split-second to raise his weapon enough to fire, but there were two problems with that. He didn't have a split-second, because that was all the man needed to pull the trigger. The other, more important point was that the man's rifle didn't move at all, because the hands holding it were rock steady.

"We were wondering how you were going to get down from there," the man said, and Keo saw something that looked like pale lips smiling behind the layer of mud and dirt that covered his face.

Wait. Did the man just say *we?*

Snap! A branch broke under a heavy boot behind him.

Keo didn't turn around. He couldn't, even if he wanted to, not with the rifle pointing at him. Any little move, and he was likely a dead man. The fact that he was still alive was confusing. Why was he still alive? Did Pollard want him unharmed? What was that Fiona had said?

"Pollard was willing to just kill you when you were out there running around. But now that you're cornered, he'll want more. He'll demand his pound of flesh. He'll want to take his time with the two of you because he can afford to now."

Keo could smell the second man before he heard or felt the barrel of his rifle tapping against the back of his neck. "You're a long way from home," the second man said. "You speak English?"

"Yeah," Keo said.

"Say something else."

"Something else."

Chuckling. "Smartass, huh?"

Keo bit his tongue and didn't answer that one.

"You got a name?" the man behind him asked.

"Keo," he said.

"What kind of name is Keo?"

"Larry was taken."

CHAPTER 6

"WHAT ARE YOU doing out here, smartass?"

That was the smaller one, who walked behind Keo, while the bigger one led the way.

They had been going west for the last five minutes, and neither man was in any particular hurry. Keo couldn't figure out how they had gotten the drop on him. From what he could tell, they had been in the woods for a while, given the ghillie suits both men were wearing. The mud and dirt on them also looked fresh.

Quiet as mice. With rifles.

Had they really been in the area all night, hiding in plain sight? It was a crazy thought *(absolutely bonkers)*, but what other explanation was there?

The one in front of him was about six feet tall, and the thick ghillie suit made him appear twice his size. He was cradling a rifle that looked like a modern version of the Browning light machinegun, but more importantly, the scope on top of it would have made shooting Keo at twenty meters child's play. He couldn't tell the man's age with all the junk over his face, but he guessed he was somewhere in his forties. The man carried himself well, moving with a smoothness only possible for someone used to being out here.

The one behind him was younger by at least twenty years. Keo could tell that much from just his voice, never mind the annoying personality. Like the older one, the ghillie suit hid most of his features, but it didn't hide the camo rifle he was pointing at Keo's back from a meter away at the moment. That was just far enough to keep him from trying anything, but close enough that he could hear his captor's breathing. The man had Keo's MP5SD, along with the Glock .45 and the Ka-Bar, stuffed into the now mostly-empty pack.

He was in an impossible situation between the two of them, with a big unknown waiting ahead of him. Still, he might have taken his chances and tried to escape anyway…if they hadn't bound his hands together at the wrists with zip ties.

The one bright spot that he could see was that they weren't Pollard's men. He knew that much right away. Pollard's people had a uniform—black assault vests and camo face paint—but they didn't do ghillie suits. These men hadn't shot him on sight (another big plus), and they seemed almost amused by the fact that he had climbed down from the tree this morning.

"How'd you get up there?" the man behind him asked.

"The tree?" Keo said.

"No, the Empire State Building. Yeah, the tree."

Keo smiled. "I climbed."

"That's one hell of a climb."

"I'm a very good climber."

"No kidding, Rain Man."

"I don't know what that means."

"You know, from the movie *Rain Man* with Tom Cruise?"

"I've never seen that movie."

"It was pretty good. I think that short guy might have won an award for it or something."

"Tom Cruise?"

"No, the other short guy."

"Dustin Hoffman," the big one in front of them said.

"Yeah, him," the second one said.

"I don't watch a lot of movies," Keo said.

"Yeah, I got that," the short one said.

"Where are we going?"

"Hey, which one of us has the guns here?"

"You."

"That's right. So we ask the questions, and you answer. See how this works?"

"Well, now that you've clarified it, sure."

The older one chuckled. "This guy is funnier than you, Shorty."

"Easy to be funny when you're trying not to fall asleep in a tree," the one named Shorty said.

They definitely saw me up there before sunrise.

How is that possible?

Keo heard a squawk, and the man in front of him reached into the folds of his ghillie suit and pulled out a two-way radio just as a female voice said, "Zachary, come in. Over."

"Everything okay?" the man named Zachary said into the radio.

"Everything's fine over here. What about out there? Shorty?"

"He's in one piece."

"Tell her I'm starving," Shorty said.

"He says he misses you and wants to touch you in inappropriate places when we get back," Zachary said.

Shorty snorted. "Two smartasses today."

"I bet," the woman said through the radio. "What about those guys you saw all over the park? We heard a lot of shooting yesterday. It sounded like some kind of war was going on over there."

"It was close," Zachary said. "We're bringing over a guy who'll be able to provide some answers. He's a real talker."

"Who is it?"

"Said his name's Keo."

"What kind of name is Keo?"

"Apparently because every other name in the English language was taken."

Keo grinned.

"What's wrong?" Zachary said into the radio.

"What do you mean?" the woman said.

"Come on. You sound pissed off."

"You and Shorty, staying out there again. I told you before, it's too dangerous. You need to stop taking unnecessary risks like that."

"Couldn't be helped. We got caught outside. Nothing you can do about it but roll with the punches."

"I don't want to argue," the woman said. "Just get back here."

"Will do. Over." Zachary put the radio away.

"Who was that?" Keo asked. "Your wife? She sounds angry."

"Allie," Zachary said.

"He wishes she was his wife," Shorty said. "Hell, I wish she was my wife."

"She didn't sound very happy with the two of you," Keo said.

"It's her job to worry," Zachary said. "She's the boss. But I think she'll get over it when I bring you back. I'm sure she has a lot of questions. You guys freaked everyone out with your shooting."

"So, she's the boss? Allie?"

"Pretty much."

"Not bad looking, either," Shorty said. "Too bad she's a lesbian."

"She's not a lesbian," Zachary said.

"I've been trying to get with her for months now. Trust me, she plays for the other team."

Zachary snorted. "Just 'cause she doesn't want to sleep with you doesn't mean she's a lesbian, Shorty. That would make the vast majority of the female population lesbians even before they got turned into bloodsuckers."

Shorty wasn't convinced. "Lesbian. One hundred percent."

THEY LED HIM through the woods for another thirty minutes. It would have been faster, but Zachary began doubling back before taking different turns the second time through the same path. Or, at least, he thought it was the same direction. He couldn't really be sure, which told him Zachary was doing a damn good job. What he did know for sure was that he was dealing with seasoned trackers and woodsmen here.

Great. I got captured by Daniel Boone and his little buddy.

Even Shorty seemed to know what he was doing, and the two communicated with looks instead of words. That was, when they needed to "talk" at all. After the initial burst of conversation, neither one had said another word to him.

Instead of engaging them in conversation, Keo waited patiently for his opportunity. Unfortunately, between Shorty's steady rifle at his back and Zachary's calm pace in front of him, he never saw anything that he could have even confused for an opening.

Damn, they're too good.

He was already sweating under the morning heat despite the plentiful shade, but neither of his two captors appeared to share his discomfort despite what they were wearing. He found that slightly annoying but refrained from saying so. They hadn't shown any indications they were the enemy, but that could easily change at a moment's notice. Right now, he was still breathing, and he wanted to keep it that way.

After another ten minutes of walking, Zachary turned left, and Keo heard waves lapping, so he guessed they were close to the shore. He wasn't sure how they had gotten here, but apparently this was the destination all along.

Zachary stopped at some bushes, grabbed a large branch, and pulled, revealing a dull gray canoe about fourteen feet long and thirty-five inches wide. It looked long enough for three people (with extra room for even a fourth), and there were two paddles inside and a mount in the back for a trolling motor to be attached.

"We going swimming?" Keo asked.

"Something like that," Zachary said.

"You can swim if you want," Shorty said. "We'll just pull

you along the side. Howzabout it, funny guy?"

"I guess I can go for a canoe ride," Keo said.

"You guys don't swim where you're from?"

"I'm mostly from San Diego."

"No kidding."

"Nope."

"Never been to San Diego. Nice?"

"I said I lived there for a time; I didn't marry it."

"Smartass," Shorty said, but he chuckled anyway.

The canoe was light enough that Zachary could handle it by himself. He slung his rifle and grabbed one end, then dragged it out of the woods and onto a small stretch of beach. The polyethylene hull scraped against pebbles and debris as it slid easily across the small patch of land before slipping into the warm lake water.

"You get middle seat," Zachary said. "Lucky you, we're going to be doing all the paddling."

"A free boat ride?" Keo said. "My day's looking up."

He felt a little clumsy climbing into the canoe with his hands bound, but he managed to grab onto the side and pulled himself in, the long but narrow vessel moving dangerously under him.

He tried to remember the last time he had been on a boat. Years, probably. He had always been a strong swimmer, thanks to all those summers hanging around Mission Beach. Or, when the tourist throngs became too much to bear, there was always Pacific Beach. Ironically, while he could swim with the best of them (and better than most), Keo had never been a particularly good boater. He knew, as the saying went, just enough to get in trouble.

Once Keo was inside, Shorty climbed up front while Zachary pushed off before hopping into the back. They each grabbed a paddle and started stroking, the canoe gliding smoothly across the calm lake surface. Keo was hoping it would be cooler out here in the water, but five minutes in and he was still sweating from the heat.

"Are we going to the other side?" Keo asked.

"You'll see," Shorty said. "Just relax and enjoy the ride, San Diego."

"That's going to be a little hard to do. My friend is still out there. He needs my help."

It had taken Keo a while to understand why Norris had run off on him yesterday. Norris had done the right thing, giving their pursuers two targets instead of just one. It was the smart move, and if Keo had been thinking clearly that day, he would have agreed with Norris when the older man made the suggestion. But he hadn't, which had forced Norris to take it upon himself to split them up.

Keo didn't know whether to curse Norris or thank him for taking the initiative that, probably, saved both their lives. Of course, he'd need to find the ex-cop first in order to do either one. Right now, Norris could be dead or dying, or captured. Too many possibilities, all of them highly possible.

"You mean the black guy," Zachary said behind him.

Keo looked over his shoulder. "You saw him."

"Yeah."

"Did you see what happened to him?"

"Don't know. He went north and you went west."

"You were there last night. In the woods."

Zachary nodded.

"Where were you?" Keo asked.

Zachary grinned back at him. Sweat had wiped some of the mud and dirt off his face, leaving behind something that looked like a mask made up of smeared mascara.

"In the ground?" Keo said. "Are you shitting me? Those things..."

"The bloodsuckers," Shorty said.

"Yeah, the bloodsuckers. How...?"

Shorty looked back at him. He seemed just as amused as Zachary by Keo's reaction. "Zach and me have spent all our lives out here, San Diego. We can get so close to a deer we can touch it if we want to. You don't think we can do the same to those freaks?"

Keo didn't know how to respond to that. A part of him *was* awed by what they had done last night. Not only hadn't the creatures seen them, but *he* hadn't seen them either, and he had a great view from above. They must have been there all night, watching him from somewhere on the ground in their ghillie suits.

You would love these guys, Norris. They're crazier than I am by a good mile.

"You saw me in the tree," Keo said. "How long?"

"Didn't see you climb up," Zachary said, "but saw you trying to stay awake last night."

"Best damn show I ever saw in a long time," Shorty chuckled. "Drinking water, pinching yourself, pulling your earlobes. Man, I wish I had one of those GoPro cameras. Put you on YouTube or something. I'd probably get a million hits."

"How did they not see you?" Keo asked.

"They came close," Zachary said. He looked suddenly

thoughtful. "I was pretty sure a couple of the devils had spotted me. Or smelled me, at least."

Keo remembered the two bloodsuckers from last night. The two that had stopped and sniffed the air for a moment before racing off again. He had thought they had smelled *him*, but it was actually Zachary all this time.

"They almost did," Keo said.

"Yeah," Zachary said, and gave Keo a *Whew!* grin. "That was a close one."

"Eyes forward, San Diego," Shorty said. "We're home."

Keo turned around and stared at "home."

It was an island.

A small island, anyway. It didn't take him very long to see all of it because there wasn't that much of it to see. Half a football field, he guessed, with most of it taken up with trees and a brown stretch of beach up front. There were makeshift camps spread out across the open spaces, filled up with a dozen tents of varied colors and sizes. Almost as many people were moving around, some coming from the wooded area behind them carrying branches that they deposited into permanent campfires. A couple of men looked up from one of those fires, and Keo got a whiff of burning fish.

There were two wooden docks sticking out of the center of the island, with the biggest vessel by far tied up to one of them. It looked more like a floating RV than an actual boat. A houseboat of some sort, designed specifically to spend more time on the water than on dry land. The rest of the dock space was filled up with boats of various shapes and sizes. They looked permanently fastened to the docks while another dozen or so were anchored just off the island. There were people on some of the boats, especially the ones with cabins, though he received a few curious glances from a pontoon boat.

Keo remembered moving along the shoreline a few days ago, going through the expensive lakeside homes, and not finding a single boat parked in the water.

Not even a life raft, he remembered thinking. *Where did all the boats go?*

Here, apparently. They all came here.

"The supplies from the houses," Keo said, looking back at Zachary. "You guys took them. The water, nonperishable food, weapons..."

"Most of them," Zachary nodded. "We got all the weapons we need, so we dumped most of them into the lake. Too dangerous to just leave behind."

"For who?"

"Us. We don't know you from Adam, kid."

"Gotta look after our own," Shorty said. "Boss's orders."

"This Allie?" Keo said.

"Yup," Zachary said. "That's her over there."

A tall African-American woman had come out of the cabin of the houseboat and was climbing over the side railing and onto the dock. He couldn't tell how old she was from the distance, but she looked comfortable in cargo pants and a white T-shirt, and she was raising a radio to her lips just before Zachary's own radio squawked in the back of the canoe.

"Any trouble?" the woman, Allie, asked through the radio.

"We made sure no one saw us pushing off," Zachary said. "You worry too much."

"If I'm not worrying, you should be, Zach. We just put some fish on the grill for you guys."

"Much appreciated."

"Don't say I never did anything for you."

Keo looked back at Zachary. "I need to get back to land. My friend is still out there. You understand loyalty, don't you?"

"I do," Zachary said, but then shook his head. "But it's not up to me. You'll have to talk to Allie."

"So, she's really in charge."

"Yup. She's really in charge."

"Girl power, and all that," Shorty chuckled in front of him.

"That, and she's smarter than the rest of us," Zachary said.

"That's a matter of opinion," Shorty said.

Allie had walked up the wooden planks to the end of the dock and was waiting for them as they coasted toward her. Two men, both in their twenties, had appeared alongside her at the same time. One of them grabbed a rope and tossed it over to Shorty, while the other man, a redhead, stood back with a hunting rifle cradled in his arms, eyeing Keo.

"This him?" Allie said.

"That's him," Shorty said. "Mister San Diego."

"Keo," Zachary said, "this is Allie."

Allie looked him up and down, and he took the opportunity to do the same to her. Early thirties, attractive, about five-seven, and with clearly intelligent eyes. The kind of woman who would have intimidated him in a bar, though of course that wouldn't have chased him away.

"You wanna tell me what you and your friends were doing running around the park, shooting it up?" she asked.

"They're not my friends," Keo said.

"Then who are they?"

"What do you call people trying to murder you?"

Allie frowned. "Do they have a reason?"

"Depends on your perspective."

She looked past him at Zachary. "He sounds like trouble, Zach. You should have saved us the trouble and just shot him and tossed his body in the lake."

"Still not too late for that," Shorty said, climbing out of the canoe. "It's a big lake."

My big mouth, Keo thought, and said quickly, "I was told you had questions, then you'll let me go."

She narrowed her eyes. "We'll see."

CHAPTER 7

"HOW MANY ARE we talking about?" Allie asked.

"I saw around ten," Keo said.

"But that's not all of them."

"No."

"Stop beating around the bush. How many more are running around the park right now with machine guns?"

"Assault rifles."

"What?"

"They're carrying around mostly assault rifles. I haven't seen a machine gun among them yet."

"What's the difference?"

"Well, machine guns are—"

"I don't care," she interrupted. "How many more?"

He smiled. "I was told around fifty."

"That's a lot."

"Yup."

He followed her the short distance from the dock to the houseboat. It was beige, just over forty feet long and somewhere around fifteen feet wide. There were already a couple of people onboard, including one man inside the long cabin in the middle. The second one was manning a gas grill at one corner of the foredeck. Keo smelled more cooking fish and licked his lips.

"Hungry?" Allie said.

"I've been surviving on plants, MREs, rain water, and dirt for the last few months."

"Lucky you, we have plenty of fish to share."

"What kind of fish?"

"The cooked kind. You on a diet?"

"Seafood diet. You know what that is?"

"What am I, five years old?"

"You don't look five, no."

"Don't get too comfortable. This isn't a date. I could still toss you overboard at any moment."

"Understood."

Allie swung her long legs over the boat's railing without any trouble. Freed from the zip ties, Keo followed suit, with his new bodyguard bringing up the rear. The twenty-something redhead, Granger, had one hand permanently on the butt of his holstered Glock. Granger also had Keo's pack and MP5SD, while Zachary and Shorty had headed over to a tent somewhere along the beach.

Granger was smart enough to keep a reasonable distance, not that Keo was entertaining the idea of escaping. There was no point that he could see. Allie and her people clearly didn't intend to harm him, despite all her unveiled threats. He knew killers when he saw and heard them, and he wasn't in the company of killers here.

"How long has it been?" he asked.

"What's that?" she said, leading him along the side of the

boat, the large box-shaped cabin to their left.

"Since you guys shoved off land."

"About one week after the world stopped making sense. We initially had just this one houseboat, but we added the others as more people showed up over the next few weeks and months."

"Whose idea was this?"

"Mine." They reached the foredeck, where Allie pointed to the man standing in front of a metal grill rooted to the boat. Fish sizzled, and the smell made Keo's mouth water some more. "That's Bill. Bill, this is Keo."

Bill, who looked to be in his fifties, gave him a perfunctory nod. "What kind of name is Keo?"

"Jimmy was taken," Keo said.

Allie smirked. "That's a running gag with you?"

"I don't know what you're talking about."

"Whatever. Follow me."

She led him into the cabin, which was surprisingly spacious. A man in Bermuda shorts and a Hawaiian shirt, sitting in the officer's chair in front of the helm reading a magazine, stood up and shook his hand when they entered.

"Gabe, Keo. Keo, Gabe," Allie said. "Gabe's in charge of making sure the boats don't sink in the middle of the night."

"She's exaggerating my qualifications," Gabe said. "I'm just a beach bum."

Gabe was in his early forties and probably a little too tanned for his own good. Keo wondered if that was an issue with the people here, with the sun always beating down on top of them with only the tents and cabins for cover.

"You staying a while?" Gabe asked.

"Not if I can help it," Keo said.

"We'll see about that," Allie said, and gave him a long look. "You could use a little cleaning up."

"Is that some kind of subtle hint?"

"I didn't know I was being subtle." She wrinkled her nose. "You can use that room," she said, pointing to the back room. "That's also where I and others sleep, so don't touch anything. I'll get Granger to bring you some spare clothes, and we'll talk over fish when you're done."

"You have a working shower in there?"

She laughed. "No, genius. Use the lake, like the rest of us. Then you can change in there. Unless, of course, you like letting everything hang out."

HE SWAM AROUND the island for the next ten minutes, washing every part of him with a bar of soap that Granger had tossed over while the redhead stood along the side of Allie's houseboat doing his best not to look. The others had also courteously stopped gawking, though some of the kids couldn't resist.

He changed into new cargo pants and a T-shirt in the back room, which took up one quarter of the cabin and held bunk beds. There were dressers, but apparently not enough for everyone, judging by the clothes hanging along wall hooks. Women's clothes.

Allie and the others, including Gabe and Bill, and a bearded forty-something Keo hadn't seen before, sat around the dining table in the center of the cabin eating fried fish with their hands when he came back out. It took Keo a few seconds to realize the bearded man was actually Zachary, cleaned up and wearing regular clothes.

"Look at you," Allie said. "Cleaned up real good."

"Was that a compliment?" Keo said.

"Mostly, sure."

The others made room for him to sit at the table. Allie tossed a fried white bass onto a ceramic plate from a big basket at the center of the table and slid it over in front of him. His fingers were almost trembling when he picked it up and started eating.

Jesus, it tasted good.

"So, you want to tell us what's going on out there?" Allie said. "It sounded like you guys were fighting World War III."

"You can hear all the way out here?" Keo said.

"You'd have to be deaf not to. Sound travels these days. Plus, Zach has been tracking all of it since…when?"

"About nine days ago," Zachary said. "Faded shots, but it was pretty clear they were coming our way. Shorty and I came to the conclusion they've been chasing you and your friend since that first gunshot. We wrong?"

Keo shook his head. "No."

"Who are they?" Allie said. "The truth."

Keo spent a moment digesting the fish. It was slightly overcooked and crunched in his mouth, but it still tasted better than anything he'd had in…well, it had been a while. Allie opened a cooler and took out a bottle of water. It tasted like rain.

"We're running from a guy named Pollard," Keo said. "He wants to kill us."

"Why?" Allie asked.

"Because I killed his son."

Allie stared at him for a moment. Then she exchanged a

look with Zachary, then with Bill and Gabe. He could almost see her mind turning, crunching the numbers to see how much trouble he had brought them, and how putting a bullet in his head, then tossing him into the lake would solve all her troubles. His first instinct was that she wasn't capable of something like that, but that was before the world went to shit. Who knew, these days, what even the most mild-mannered person was capable of...

"Why did you kill his son?" she finally asked.

"Because his son was trying to kill me," Keo said.

"So it was self-defense."

"Yes."

"Or is that your interpretation of events?"

"What is this, a courtroom?"

"Why shouldn't it be?" she said with a slight edge in her voice.

"He didn't give me any choices. He was trying to shoot me, so I shot him first."

"Sounds pretty straightforward."

"It was."

"From the beginning," Zachary said. "The truth, kid."

Keo told them about the attack on the house and killing Joe during the gunfight. He skipped the part about Levy, the creature in the garage, and Bobby, Pollard's nephew. He told them about Gillian and the others escaping on Mark's boat during the battle, then added in the ambush by Pollard's men at the gas station along the interstate, figuring it would get him some bonus points. He left out the part where he and Norris killed two more of Pollard's men at the barbershop.

Nothing he told them was a lie. He just elected not to tell

them everything. Given their situation—hiding out here in the middle of the lake—he guessed (hopefully correctly) that they were more apt to fall on his side if forced to choose between him and a man like Pollard.

"So they just go around taking what they want?" Gabe said when Keo finished.

"They have the firepower for it," Keo said. "From what I've been told, Pollard is ex-military, and he's leading the others like a paramilitary group."

"How do they survive out there?" Allie asked. "Do they have a base?"

"Apparently there are more of them back in Corden. Pollard just bought his killers with him. As for how they've been surviving since they started chasing us, I guess the same way we have—sheltering in buildings at nights, et cetera."

"Hard to do with that many people," Zachary said.

"Not my problem. I got the impression they were used to it, though."

"Would have to be. Fifty is a lot of people to take care of on the road."

Keo grabbed another bass and dug out some choice white meat. He was thinking about Norris as he ate.

Are you still alive out there, old-timer?

"So, what's your next move?" Allie asked him.

"Go back and find my friend," Keo said.

"What if he's dead? Or captured?"

"Doesn't matter. I need to find out for sure. I owe him."

Allie nodded. "Okay."

"Okay?" he said.

"Okay," she said again. Then, "We'll return your stuff and

you can be on your way. I assume you'll want to leave as soon as possible."

"You assumed correctly." Then he added, "Thanks."

"Don't bother. The only reason we even believe anything you're saying is because of what Zachary and Shorty saw out there. They backed up your story of this Pollard asshole having a paramilitary army running around in the park."

"You saw them?" Keo said to Zachary.

Zachary nodded. "They made base at the visitors' building at the other side of the park. Like you said, about fifty or so. Tactical assault gear and armed to the teeth. People like that are used to taking what they want."

"So eat up, and I'll send Zachary and Shorty to take you back to the park," Allie said.

He smiled at her. "And, of course, me going back there keeps you out of Pollard's crosshairs in case he notices your little island out here, right?"

"What, was I being too subtle again?" Allie said.

HE WOULD HAVE liked to spend more time on the island, maybe get to know the other survivors and pick up supplies they might be willing to part with, but time wasn't on his side at the moment.

Big surprise. Time, you're such a bitch.

So he spent the next few minutes after lunch (or was it breakfast?) in the back room making sure the MP5SD was still working after it had been manhandled first by Shorty, then Granger. He dry fired it before loading it back up.

Allie came in while he was counting his magazines and checking the Glock. "Got enough bullets there?"

He smiled over. "You can never have too many bullets."

"Good to hear. Wouldn't want you to run up against this Pollard asshole without the proper tools at your disposal."

"That would be a crying shame, all right."

She hesitated, and he sensed she was about to say something but wasn't quite sure how to do it.

"What's on your mind, Allie?"

"You can stay here," she said, "if you wanted."

"I thought you were anxious for me to leave."

"You can always come back later. As long as we stay under Pollard's radar, he'll eventually have to move on."

"Thanks, I appreciate it, but I made a promise."

"To your friend."

"To him, and to someone else, too. That means heading south after all this is over." *If I'm still alive,* he thought, but added instead, "But thanks for the offer. It's tempting."

"Too bad," she said, then turned to go.

"How'd you know?"

She looked back. "About what?"

"The island. How'd you know the bloodsuckers couldn't swim?"

"I didn't. We needed a place to go and some of the people I was sheltering with in the early days knew about this place. We only learned later that they didn't like the water. After that, it just made sense to stay here. We've been here for almost a year, and we haven't run out of homes to raid for supplies yet. It's going to be a long time before we even have to risk going farther inland."

"It's a good setup," he nodded. "You guys have a good thing going here."

"We were lucky."

"I've been wondering since I arrived at the park, but whose idea was it to bring all the boats over?"

"All? You've only been to a small piece of the lake, Keo. The boats you see here don't represent all the ones that were left behind. We only took the ones that we could use."

"What about the rest?"

"We sank them."

"All of them?"

"Haven't you learned by now? The creatures are dangerous at night, but there are other dangerous species in the day."

"Guys like Pollard."

"Ding ding, give the man with the questionable name a prize."

He chuckled. "Cute."

"Hey, I'm a former divorce lawyer. I'll take that as a compliment."

"Divorce lawyer. Ouch."

"Only if you weren't one of my clients."

"I was never the marrying kind myself."

"No, but you're the loyal kind. Going back there is suicide, but you're doing it anyway. That's impressive."

"Thanks," he said, "because I'm pretty sure I'm the biggest dumbass in the universe."

She laughed. "Hey, there are no rules that say I can't think you're the biggest dumbass in the universe and still respect you."

✳

SHORTY, LIKE ZACHARY, had changed into civilian clothes when Keo saw him again, though like his older companion, he was as heavily armed as the first time they had met. Both men were waiting in the canoe when he walked down the dock by himself and climbed in.

"You must have a death wish or something, San Diego," Shorty said.

"He's going to look for a friend," Zachary said. "Can't blame the man."

"Sure I can. Just watch me."

Keo settled into the same spot in the middle of the boat while Shorty pushed them off with his paddle. The two men turned them around then began stroking back toward land. Keo glanced over one shoulder and saw Allie on the deck of the houseboat looking in their direction. She wasn't the only one. Curious strangers poked their heads out of tents, and some stood on boat decks to watch him go.

That's right, boys and girls, get a look at the dumbest man in the known universe. He will wow you with his stupid decisions.

He turned around and faced the shoreline. The trees looked small in the distance, like blades of grass sticking out of an untended front yard. "Has anyone ever spotted the island from the shore?" he asked.

"It's happened once or twice," Zachary said. "It's a lot harder than you'd think, even with binoculars, unless you know exactly where to look."

No one said anything else for the next twenty minutes. The only noise was the soothing *whoosh-whoosh* of the paddles cutting through the water in front and behind, and to the left and right of him. Keo took the time to reorient himself with the shape of the park. It looked different when viewed from the middle of the lake. Longer and more expansive somehow. And it had felt pretty damn huge when he was racing through it before.

They were about 200 meters from land when Zachary said, "Stop for a moment, Shorty."

Keo looked back at Zachary, who picked up a gym bag from the bottom of the boat and handed it to him. "Allie thought you might be able to use it. Just in case."

Keo took the bag—it was heavy—and opened it. He looked in at an M4 rifle with a holographic gun sight on top. He also counted six spare magazines and two bottles of water.

"Those should keep you going for a while in case that German gun quits on you," Zachary said.

"She must like you," Shorty said from the front. Then, in a lower voice, "Maybe she's not a lesbian after all."

Keo ignored him and said to Zachary, "Thank Allie for me when you get back."

"I'll do that," Zachary said. He picked up his paddle and dipped it back into the water.

Shorty did likewise, and the canoe started moving again, taking them closer to land with every stroke.

Back toward Pollard and his fifty men.

Back to Norris…if he was even still alive.

CHAPTER 8

HE KNEW WHERE the island was—or, at least, its general direction—but Keo still couldn't see it with the naked eye no matter how hard he tried. He guessed it might be different if he had a pair of binoculars. He could see the canoe, though; it was a tiny dot in the horizon, with Zachary and Shorty two stick figures seemingly floating on top of the water.

Keo turned and hurried off the beach and into the woods, hefting the gym bag with the M4 over one shoulder, the MP5SD in front of him. It was still an hour before noon, but the heat was already making a menace of itself. He couldn't imagine how much worse it would have been if he hadn't taken a dip in the lake earlier and was still trudging around in his old dirt, mud, and blood-covered clothes.

He had to find Norris.

He didn't know how. That was the problem. His best option—his *only* option—was to head back to the two-story house along the eastern shoreline and try to pick up the trail from there. Zachary had put him back on land about the same place they had taken off from, so all he had to do was backtrack and keep the lake to his right just beyond the tree lines.

If all else failed, he knew where Pollard's base was. Of course, that was a worst-case scenario. As much as he wanted to find Norris—and save him, if he needed saving—the idea of going up against fifty (or so) men wasn't exactly something he eagerly embraced. Keo was used to bad odds, but damn, these were *really* bad odds.

He walked for an hour, maintaining a steady pace, and only drank half the bottle of water he had transferred from the gym bag to his pack. If he had to run, the bag and the heavy M4 in it, not to mention the spare magazines, would have to go first. He would have loved to be able to carry both weapons, but if push came to shove, the MP5SD was always his first choice. No one made weapons like the Germans.

It was just past noon when he finally got close enough to the two-story house to spot its familiar white frame from a distance. He knew it wasn't empty when he was still 200 meters away because he could hear voices. They weren't being very quiet.

Keo went into a crouch and listened to a conversation in mid-stream. A man and a woman, less than sixty meters in front of him, hidden from him just like he was hidden from them (or at least, he hoped). It was a miracle they hadn't heard his approach.

It took another ten seconds of listening before he realized they weren't actually talking. The sounds he heard weren't words, but moaning, grunting, and sighs of pleasure.

Daebak. Now I'm a pervert, too.

He stood up slightly and began to backtrack.

Soon, the sounds of sex drifted away into the woods. He hoped they at least used some kind of blanket before they got down to it. It would have been a shame if they got a rash, or an infection, or something equally regretful while doing the nasty.

End of the world, boys and girls. Get it while you can.

When he had put enough distance between himself and the lovers, Keo relaxed and turned north, and this time he was more aware of the noises he was making. He should have been more careful earlier, too. All it would have taken was one pair of attentive ears and he would have been a dead man back there. It would have been hard to rescue Norris with a bullet in his head.

That is, if Norris needed rescuing at all. He'd find out when he found the ex-cop. That, unfortunately, was easier said than done.

He took a quick look down at his watch: 12:24 P.M.

At least he had plenty of time…

HE CIRCLED THE clearing around the house, trying to pick up Norris's tracks from when they had fled into the woods the day earlier while still keeping as far away from the tree lines as possible. The last thing he needed was to run into another amorous couple doing the nasty during their lunch break. He crossed a couple of limited hiking trails, two of many that snaked all around the park.

The world of green and brown and sunlight around him looked, sounded, and felt empty, as if he could walk for days without actually running across another human being.

It was a hopeless task, and he wondered how he ever convinced himself that this was even a possibility. There were no obvious signs of Norris, and whatever prints had been created in the soft ground the previous day had been trampled by hundreds *(thousands)* of bare feet last night. The creatures. The bloodsuckers. They were simply everywhere, though the fact that he couldn't see them now, in the daylight, made him slightly nervous.

After a while, he decided to stop deluding himself and turned north, in the direction that he always knew he would end up eventually: the park visitors' building at the entrance, which Pollard was using as his base of operations. With his fifty or so people...

Shit, that's a lot of guns.

If Norris had been captured, he would be there right now, because Pollard wouldn't kill him right away. At least, he hoped not. Which was an odd thing to be hoping for, but at the moment it was the better of two options.

If Norris wasn't there, then that meant he was still roaming around the woods. That was a much better outcome, but problematic because it meant Keo would have to go looking for the old-timer. Still, Norris out there was better than Norris in captivity. Would Pollard care it was him, and not the ex-cop, that had killed his son? Maybe, maybe not.

Either way, he had to know for sure.

From his time in Robertson Park, Keo knew there were three main roads that forked from the entrance. The people who made use of the park were mostly hikers, fishermen, and the people who owned the lakeside homes. All the parking lots were located near the southern shore, and the rest were pretty much dense wooded areas—

Crunch-crunch!

Two figures. Black-clad. Walking across his path twenty

meters away.

Keo slipped behind a tree, the gym bag with the rifle and spare magazines *clanking* against his back.

Too loud.

He knew they had heard him as soon as he heard the *clanking* himself. He muttered a silent curse and spun away from the tree, lifted the MP5SD, and peered through the sight at the two figures just as they were turning, reacting too slowly to the noise.

They froze at the sight of him, the steel barrel of the suppressor pointing in their direction. He had them dead to rights and they knew it.

There were two of them. A man and a woman. Except the man wasn't really a man. He was a kid carrying an M4 and looked out of place covered up with all the tactical gear and ammo pouches. He was way too young to be staring wide-eyed at Keo with a face that, for just a split-second, reminded Keo of Joe and Bobby.

Fucking Joe. You lying punk.

But it wasn't the face that Keo saw clearly across the short distance that separated them. It was the eyes. They telegraphed what the kid was about to do before he did it.

Oh, you little bastard, you're going to make me kill you, aren't you? Keo thought, and started to squeeze the trigger just as the kid began lifting his rifle, even though he knew *(he knew!)* that Keo had him sighted down.

That was when the woman whirled on the boy and smashed the stock of her rifle into his back. The kid let out a surprised grunt and stumbled forward. The woman followed and delivered a second vicious hit to the back of his head. This time, the teenager fell to the ground and lay still on his stomach.

"Don't shoot," the woman said, raising her hands into the air.

Keo stared across at the familiar face. It wasn't covered in paint this time, not that he would have mistaken her for anyone else even if it had been. He would remember those blue eyes anywhere.

"Don't shoot," Fiona said again. "Come on, you haven't forgotten me already, have you, Keo?"

"No," Keo said.

He didn't lower his weapon though. Keo was still trying to understand what the hell just happened. Did she just knock out one of her own? Why?

"Come on, Keo," Fiona said. "My arm is killing me. You remember what happened to it, don't you?"

He lowered the submachine gun a bit. "Stop whining. It was just a scratch."

"God, you're an ass." Relieved, Fiona put down her arms with a painful grimace.

"I need that," he said.

"What?"

"Your rifle."

She sighed and tossed it into the grass in front of him.

"The sidearm, too," Keo said.

She tossed it as well.

"How's the shoulder?" he asked.

"It hurts like a sonofabitch every time I move it. How do you think it is?"

He looked down at the unconscious body. "What was that about?"

"You would have shot him."

"That doesn't answer my question."

"I don't want you to shoot him. He's a good kid. He's just…not that bright."

"You know him?"

"I know all of them. I've been with Pollard for eight months. We've eaten, slept, and hell, I've even fucked a couple of them."

"Just a couple?"

She smirked. "What else is there to do these days? Can't even waste time on Twitter or Facebook anymore. What's the world coming to?"

She crouched and felt the boy's neck, and satisfied that he was still alive, touched the sticky patch at the back of his head.

Keo kept a close eye on her. There was a fifty-fifty percent chance she might go for the boy's sidearm or the fallen M4 a few feet away. Keo had purposefully not collected those. He wanted to see what she would do.

"Still alive?" Keo asked.

"Yes." She wiped her bloody palm against the grass and made a face. "God, I hope I didn't give him brain damage."

"You hit him with the stock of your rifle. He'll be fine." *Mostly,* he thought, but didn't bother to add that part.

Keo looked around him to make sure their little incident hadn't drawn more attention from the rest of Pollard's men. He went quiet and listened but didn't hear any footsteps running toward them.

"You're looking for him," Fiona said. She hadn't reached for the boy's rifle or sidearm, and she didn't seem interested in doing so. "Your friend. What's his name?"

"Norris."

"Right. That's why you're back here scouting the house. Trying to pick up his tracks, I guess."

"Something like that. You know where he is?"

"He's alive," she said, and gave him a sympathetic look. "Pollard has him. He's had him since yesterday."

THE KID'S NAME was Rupert. He was seventeen and had joined Pollard's group six months earlier.

"We found him and his sister hiding in a cellar near Corden," Fiona said. "They'd been there since all of this began. They managed to survive by raiding farmhouses around the area, then started coming into town when supplies ran low. I think he joined just so his sister didn't have to go to sleep starving at nights."

"How old is she?" Keo asked.

"Seventeen too, I think."

"And he takes care of them? Pollard?"

"Pollard does one thing very well—he gets you to commit to him. Before you know it, you think you owe him everything. Your trust, your loyalty, even your obedience."

"How does he do that?"

"He gives you food. Shelter. Friends. These days, that's everything."

Keo nodded. He understood what she was saying. Maybe he might have managed to carry on by himself after the world went to crap, but that was a pretty big "maybe." The fact was, having Gillian and Norris made everything easier, and he sometimes doubted if he would have gotten this far without them, or even if he would have wanted to. It could get pretty damn lonely out there by yourself, especially now with most of the planet's population gone.

Well, not gone, exactly…

Fiona was staring at the unconscious Rupert, whose hands were bound behind his back with a zip tie. Fiona had treated the wet spot on the back of his head with a first aid kit from a pouch around her waist. Keo had also stuffed a handkerchief into the kid's mouth in case he woke up screaming.

They were sitting around the spot where Rupert had gone down, Keo with his back against a tree while Fiona sat next to the teenager's still form. He had her M4 leaning against the trunk next to him. She had not gone for the kid's weapon yet, which he was glad for. The last thing he wanted to do was kill her. Despite their initial meeting, he found that he liked her. She had a spirit about her that reminded him of Gillian.

Are you still alive out there, Gillian? Did you make it to Santa Marie Island?

Most of Pollard's patrols, according to Fiona, were spread out along the shoreline looking for him this morning. The fact that they hadn't spotted him when Zachary and Shorty brought him back in the canoe was a minor miracle.

"You're not wearing your war paint today," Keo said. "Neither is the kid."

"We only put them on when we know we're going into a firefight." She shrugged, looking a little embarrassed. "It's just something a group of the guys started doing, and the rest of us decided to join in. Besides, they thought you'd be nuts to return to the house. I guess you showed them, huh?"

It's unanimous. I don't have a single working brain cell in my head.

"You know why they put me with Rupert on this—according to them—pointless patrol?" Fiona asked him.

"I'm sure you're going to tell me."

"He's my punishment. For yesterday."

"This is Pollard's way of saying you shouldn't go around getting shot?"

"Mostly it's his way of saying I shouldn't have let myself be taken. He blames me for losing the two of you at the house. If I wasn't up there on the second floor being held hostage, the others would have assaulted with everything they had and taken you and Norris before he arrived." She sighed. "So yeah, I guess he does blame me."

"At least he didn't tie you outside to a tree and leave you out there at night."

She smirked. "It was probably because I got shot in the arm. I guess that gave me some extra bonus points or something, showed him that I at least put up a fight."

"You're welcome."

"Up yours."

He chuckled before getting serious again. "What kind of shape is Norris in?"

"He's alive…"

"Fiona," he said, putting a little edge in his voice. "What have they been doing to him since last night?"

"Pollard wants you. He knows you killed Joe. If it had been Norris, he would have killed your friend last night."

"Norris told him it was me?"

"He didn't have a choice. Pollard has people with him that know how to get information." She shook her head. "Your friend's in bad shape, Keo."

Keo didn't reply right away. He didn't doubt anything she was saying, and he hadn't expected Norris to hold out under interrogation. Keo had seen twenty-somethings with bulging muscles break down under duress. There was no way Norris would—or *should*—have lasted.

"They're holding him at the park visitors' building?" he finally said.

She nodded. "Where else?"

"How many people are back there now?"

"Everyone who isn't patrolling the woods for you at the moment."

"How many are we talking about?"

"Thirty, probably. And almost every one of them heavily armed."

"Almost everyone? So not all of them?"

"There are some people there just for support. They're armed, but Pollard doesn't expect them to engage in gunfights."

Keo glanced down at Rupert. "How many are like him?"

"Like him?"

"Young and wet behind the ears."

"He's a rarity. Most of the ones out here with Pollard are older, and they're pretty good at this."

"'This'?"

"Taking what they want. It's a brave new world, Keo. Pollard preaches that every night. You're either with him or you're against him. With him, you get benefits. Against him, you get a bullet to the head."

Keo nodded. He hadn't expected anything less from Pollard. You didn't get to lead a band of trigger-happy survivors without being more than a little vicious. The secret to holding power for any length of time was the occasional exercise of that power. You couldn't expect to be king forever if you didn't chop off a head every now and then in the town square for everyone to see.

"Tell me something," Keo said. "Where does he get all the hardware? Grenades, assault rifles, and all that ammo. And these assault vests, tactical belts, and military equipment. I've been running around this part of the country for the last nine months, and I've never seen anything like it."

"He didn't say, but I always assumed he raided one of the army depots. Maybe Fort Damper? It's around here, isn't it? He's ex-Army, so I'm assuming he'd know where to find all the guns he needs. It's not like there's anyone around to guard them anymore."

"It's not Fort Damper."

"How do you know?"

"Someone told me it burned down the night all of this happened."

"How about Fort Polk? Is it still standing?"

"I have no idea," Keo said.

He spent the next few minutes trying to come up with a plan to save Norris that wouldn't end up with the both of them dead. He was running out of options, and Pollard had all the advantage—not to mention all the manpower and guns. Those were two very difficult things to overcome. He could probably manage to slug it out against a dozen people if he was really lucky, but twenty? Thirty?

Too many. Always too damn many...

Fiona stared at him in silence for a while until she couldn't stand it anymore. "So now what?"

"I came back for Norris. I'm not leaving without him."

"You'll never get close enough to get him back. If anything, you're just giving Pollard what he wants by going there."

Keo picked up her rifle and tossed it back to her. He didn't even know when he had decided to trust her, but at the moment, it seemed like the right thing to do. She caught it with her good arm, then picked up her handgun from the grass.

He looked down at Rupert. "He's going to be a problem."

"What do you mean?" she said.

"If I leave the two of you here, can you promise me he won't grab the radio and start blurting out where I'm going when he wakes up?"

She shook her head. "No."

Keo reached for his sidearm.

"Wait," she said. "Just…wait." She paused for a moment, then, "Maybe I can make him understand."

Keo gave her a doubtful look.

"He knows me," she continued. "I've been watching out for him and Georgette since the day they joined us. I can talk him into it."

He wasn't quite sure if she was trying to convince him or herself. Maybe a little of both.

Keo stared at her so she would understand he meant it when he said, "If he doesn't go for it, I won't have any choice. You understand?"

She nodded solemnly. "If I'm going to help you with this, you need to do something for me, too."

That took him by surprise. "I'm already letting you go."

"Just listen."

THE FIELDS OF LEMURIA   99

"Okay."

"When you leave, I want you to take me with you."

"Why?"

"Besides the fact that Pollard doesn't trust me anymore, everything has changed, most of it for the worse. Ever since his son died, he's been erratic. He uprooted half of our group—almost all of the unattached singles—from the safety of Corden to come after you and Norris. Since then, we've been on the constant move, slogging through these woods in search of you two idiots." She shook her head. "Don't get me wrong. I knew what I was getting into when I joined up, but the way he's obsessing over you, it's... Look, I don't want to be around when it all goes bad, okay? And take my word for it. It will go bad."

"It's dangerous out there, Fiona. You have to know that."

"Really, thanks for the news flash, Walter Cronkite. I know it's dangerous out there, but I'll take my chances. Besides, I'm not telling you to dump me as soon as we get out of this place. What I'm saying is, I'd like to tag along wherever you go to next. Two is better than one, right?"

"Three," Keo said. "You, me, and Norris."

"Right," she said. "You, me, and Norris. That's what I meant."

He could see on her face that she didn't believe a single word of it, so they had that in common.

CHAPTER 9

KEO GAVE FIONA space to work on Rupert, standing nearby while they talked in soft voices. Or Fiona talked, because Rupert mostly just looked confused, caught somewhere between wanting to run away, fighting Keo, and lying down and going back to sleep. Keo wasn't entirely sure if she was getting through to the kid or if she was even close.

Joe, you little punk. I should have killed you when I had the chance.

After ten minutes, Keo said, "Are we good?"

Fiona shook her head. "Give me a few more minutes."

"No," Keo said, and walked over.

Fiona glared at him, but he ignored her. Rupert looked suddenly frightened and attempted to get up, but he moved too fast and stumbled before falling back down on his butt.

"Jesus, Keo, you're scaring him," Fiona said.

Keo kept his eyes on Rupert. He really was young. In another time, another place, the kid would be in high school devoting his time to girls, sports, and picking colleges. Right now, he was wearing a grown man's assault vest, with pouches stuffed with ammo and an empty hip holster. Right now, he looked very much like Joe.

I should have shot you dead, Joe, you little prick.

Keo crouched in front of Rupert, whose eyes went immediately to the MP5SD leaning across Keo's right knee. Then those same blue eyes flickered up to Keo's face. Rupert had shaggy light brown hair and his face was dirt and mud-free, which, up close, only made him look younger than his seventeen years.

"Rupert, right?" Keo said.

The kid nodded.

"My name is Keo. Your friends have my friend. His name is Norris. Black guy. Fifties. You saw him?"

Rupert nodded again, hesitantly this time. His eyes went back to the submachine gun. Keo was close enough that he could hear Rupert's labored breathing. Next to them, Fiona stood quietly. Keo hoped she didn't try something. He would have hated to shoot her earlier, and he still would now. Not that he wouldn't do it, but he would prefer not to.

"I'm going to get him back," Keo said. "But right now, you're a nuisance. That means I have two options: Kill you now—"

Keo fired into the ground a few inches next to Rupert. The suppressed gunshot echoed slightly among the trees, but not enough to travel across the woods and alert anyone nearby or far away. That was the point of a suppressor, after all—and what Keo wanted to get across to the kid: *"I can kill you anytime, and your friends won't come running to help. Got it?"*

"—or make sure you don't run off to alert your buddies the first chance you get. So, which option would you prefer?"

Rupert continued staring at Keo, as if he was attempting to summon some non-existent courage. But he was betrayed by his hands, which trembled noticeably at his sides.

"When I shoot you, no one's going to hear it," Keo continued. "Understand?"

The kid nodded.

"You don't do what I tell you, I'm going to shoot you. You make a noise that I interpret, rightly or wrongly, as an attempt to screw me over, and I will shoot you. You even look at me cross-eyed, and I will shoot you. I don't know you from Adam. I don't give a shit that you have a sister. You even *think* about screwing me, and I will *shoot you*. Do you understand, Rupert?"

Another nod, this one coming faster—and with more emphasis—than the last few times.

"Now, get up," Keo said.

Rupert tried to get up but seemed to be having trouble getting his feet to obey. Fiona took one of his arms and helped him the rest of the way. He gave her a grateful (and nervous) half-smile that she returned.

Keo walked back and picked up Rupert's radio, then clipped it to his hip. He stuffed the boy's rifle into the gym bag before slinging it. The added weight was obvious, which was why he had decided to let Rupert lug the extra magazines around for him.

"Let's go," Keo said. "You take the lead, Fiona. We're burning daylight."

He glanced down at his watch: 1:16 P.M.

Still plenty of time…

HE SHOULD HAVE shot them. Or, at least, the boy.

But then he would have also had to shoot Fiona, because

regardless of her intentions to escape Pollard's tyrannical rule with him, she wasn't going to stand by and let him kill Rupert. He could tell that much by the way she talked to the kid.

So it was either kill them both or keep them around until he could let the boy go later. Maybe, just maybe, Fiona was right and she could convince him to keep quiet even when they reached their destination. That was a hell of a big if, though.

They had been walking silently through the woods for about twenty minutes now, moving north toward the park visitors' building the entire time. Fiona was up front, setting the pace, with Rupert walking silently behind her.

Keo kept a safe distance from the boy—at least two me-ters—just in case. He didn't think Rupert would try anything, but you could never be sure with kids. Youth made you do stupid things. Combine that with loyalty to Pollard, and it was likely he might end up having to kill the kid anyway. Keo didn't want to do that. He wasn't going to *not* do it, but he'd like to avoid it if possible. Joe's song-and-dance, and the resulting chaos, was still fresh in his mind, but he wasn't far gone enough to think that Rupert was Joe.

Suddenly Fiona stopped in front of him and dropped to one knee, her thin frame almost disappearing completely into the overgrown blades of grass around her.

Keo did likewise, but Rupert remained standing. He knew the kid wasn't doing it on purpose. He was caught off guard, his brain freezing up with indecision. So Keo leaped forward, grabbed him by the back of his vest, and dragged him down to the ground before pushing him onto his stomach. The boy wisely stayed down, his breath quickening noticeably under Keo's grip.

Fiona glanced back and locked eyes with him.

This is where she betrays me. Like Joe...

Instead, she nodded, and he returned it. She looked forward again and positioned her rifle to fire. He did the same with the MP5SD.

Or not.

The *crunch-crunch* of heavy boots on brittle leaves preceded the appearance of a two-man patrol. Black assault vests and assault rifles moved past trees, the two men talking quietly to one another. They were forty meters away but seemed to have no clue Keo, Fiona, and Rupert were there. Both men were in their twenties, and one of them was chewing loudly on a stick of beef jerky.

Keo looked down at Rupert, who had lifted his head. The kid saw the patrol, and for a moment Keo thought he might let out a scream to alert them and mentally prepared himself to blow a hole in the back of Rupert's head.

But Rupert didn't make a sound. He actually seemed to be regaining control of his breathing, too, before lowering his head back to the slightly cool earth.

Smart kid. You might actually live through this after all.

They watched in silence as the patrol walked across them, oblivious to their presence. They were moving so leisurely, in absolutely no hurry, that it seemed to take them minutes instead of the ten—possibly twenty—seconds it actually did.

When the patrol was finally out of sight, Fiona stood back up.

Keo followed, pulling Rupert off the ground by the back of his vest along with him.

"That was a close one," Fiona said, when the loud *crack!* of a rifle exploded across the woods, scattering birds and other furry animals racing across the branches above them.

Fiona jerked her head sideways even as the gunshot echoed, bouncing off the trees around them. Her body collapsed, her legs seeming to give out underneath her as if they could no longer support her weight. She was swallowed back up by the same patch of grass that had kept her hidden and saved her life only seconds ago.

Keo spun to his left as the two men who had walked past them emerged back out of the trees, rifles firing at them. Bullets *zip-zip-zipped* past his head and one slammed into the bag behind him, spinning his body slightly with the impact. One of the men had switched to full-auto and the ground came unglued around Keo, the smell of scorched foliage filling his nostrils. He dived behind the closest tree for cover, the bark exploding on the other side in a hail of bullets.

Rupert hadn't moved from his spot and was holding his hands up, shouting, "Wait, it's me, don't shoot—" just before he doubled over, grabbing at his stomach and letting out a loud, painful wail.

Keo sent a short burst at the two men. They were smartly keeping close to the trees even while they were moving forward, and they easily slipped behind cover at his return fire. Keo didn't waste more bullets on them. He turned and ran in the other direction.

Behind him, Rupert was screaming, the sound coming out of him at a surprisingly high pitch. The shooting had also stopped. Keo guessed the patrol had run out of bullets and was reloading, which would explain why no one was shooting at him as he fled.

He didn't stop to find out for sure, though, and kept running. But he was still moving too slow. Why the hell wasn't he going any faster?

Oh, right. The bag.

Keo shrugged off the thick strap and let the bag slip off his shoulder and onto the ground with a heavy *crunch*. No longer constrained by the extra weight, he picked up speed and the trees started to blur by. That was the good news. The bad news was that he no longer had two spare rifles. Then again, extra weapons weren't going to do him a damn bit of good if he were dead anyway.

Eventually, Keo couldn't hear Rupert's screams anymore. That meant the kid was either dead or in too much pain to cry out. Either way, the boy was no longer his problem. Fiona, too, was no longer in play, not after the head shot she took back there. It was too bad, because he really did like her.

Keo slowed down and slipped behind a large tree to catch his breath for the first time since—how long? A minute? Two? Five?

He kept one eye behind him and the other on the rest of the teeming woods. That was the only good (and bad) thing about Robertson Park. It was so goddamn thick that it was hard to see anything or anyone until they were almost on top of you.

He was still sucking in air when the radio *(Rupert's)* clipped to his hip squawked, and he heard a man's voice, someone new. "Patrol Seven to Base. Come in, Base."

A man answered the radio on the other end. "This is Base. We heard shooting nearby. Was that you, Seven?"

"That was us, Base," the first man said.

"Give us a sitrep. Over."

"Uh, we ran across one of our patrols, Base. Fiona and the boy from Patrol Two."

"Who were you shooting at, Seven?"

The man from Patrol Seven hesitated for a moment.

"Seven?" the man at Base said. "Who were you shooting at? Over."

"Patrol Two, Base."

"Say again?"

"We accidentally shot Patrol Two."

There was a brief pause from Base, before a second—and this time, very familiar—voice said through the radio. "Was he with them?"

Pollard.

It was the same voice from last night. Keo didn't know how he knew that he was listening to the man named Pollard, but he just knew. Maybe it was the absolute authority in the man's voice even through the radio's tiny speakers that gave it away.

"Yes, sir," Seven said.

"Did you get him?" Pollard asked.

"No, sir. He took off back south."

"And Patrol Two?"

"We, uh, accidentally shot Patrol Two, sir."

"How long ago?"

"About five minutes ago."

Five minutes? Damn. He must have been faster than he remembered. Of course, it could have just been the fear and adrenaline, too.

"What should we do, sir?" the man asked.

Pollard didn't answer right away.

"Sir?" Seven said. "What are your orders?"

"Check Patrol Two closely and tell me if they still have their radios," Pollard said.

Oh, come on, you've got to be kidding me.

"Yes, sir," Seven said.

There was a brief pause.

Five seconds. Ten...fifteen...

Then Seven came back on the radio. "One radio's missing, sir. Do you think he took it?"

Pollard didn't answer the question. Instead, he said, "I want everyone who isn't already established along the shoreline to return to Base immediately. Everyone else, hold your positions, and someone will be by later to give you the new radio frequency. Until then, I want complete radio silence."

*Sonofa*bitch. *Can I catch one fucking break?*

Then Pollard said through the radio, "Keo. I know you're listening."

He couldn't help himself. He felt the smile coming and didn't try to stop it. A guy like Pollard would have gone far in his old organization. Smart, ruthless, and most of all, completely single-minded when he set his sights on a goal.

Too bad that goal is to kill me, otherwise we could have been best pals.

"I know you're there," Pollard continued through the radio. "I want you to know that I'm going to find you. It might take a day. Or two. Maybe even a week. It doesn't matter how long it takes. I'm a patient man. But you know who doesn't have two days or a week? Your friend Norris." The radio went silent for about ten seconds before Pollard finally returned, except this time he wasn't addressing Keo when he said, "Don't be shy."

Keo braced himself, knowing full well whose voice he was going to hear next even before he actually heard it.

"Get the hell out of here, kid," Norris said through the radio. He was out of breath and in obvious pain. "Go, and don't look back. You hear me? Don't—" Norris didn't finish. He was interrupted by the sound of something solid hitting flesh, then something *(someone)* falling.

Pollard again. "He's a tough old man. But he's an old man, Keo. He's not going to last for much longer."

Keo unclipped the radio and raised it to his lips. "Pollard."

"Keo," Pollard said. "It's good to hear your voice. I was starting to think I was wrong, that you weren't smart enough to take one of the radios off my men."

Keo pushed off the tree and continued walking through the woods. The radio made too much noise, but moving at least kept him from being pinpointed by another passing patrol.

"That's a first," Keo said.

"What's that?"

"No one's ever accused me of being smarter than the average bear before."

"You don't give yourself enough credit, Keo. A man of below-average intelligence wouldn't have forced me to chase him all these months."

"Aw, I'm touched."

"What kind of name is Keo, anyway?"

"Dan was taken."

"Hunh."

"That's what Dan said."

Pollard went quiet for a moment, which made Keo's alarms go off. He looked around him, expecting a black-clad figure (or two) to rush out of the trees at any moment. The only sound, though, came from his own footsteps.

"How is all of this going to go down, Keo?" Pollard said.

"I don't know. Why don't you tell me? The way I hear it, you're the man with the plan."

"The way I see it, you're going to make me chase you for another few days. But eventually I'm going to corner you, and when that happens, I'll snuff you out. It's inevitable. I have the manpower. The firepower. And the most crucial part of all this? You're running out of real estate. There are only so many inches of this park you can hide in before I cover everything."

"Yeah, but can you cover everything before nightfall? The way *I* see it, you can only search for me in the daylight. After all, we both know we don't own the night anymore, don't we?"

"No, we certainly don't." A slight pause, then, "There is another option. One that will put an end to this and make both of our lives easier. Mine more than yours, of course, but I think you can see the benefit in it too if you look hard enough."

"I'm listening…"

"I don't want Norris. I want you."

"How sweet."

Pollard might have chuckled. "Let me finish."

"Go on…"

"I'm willing to let Norris live if you walk over to me, at, say, five this afternoon."

Keo stopped walking.

"It's a good offer," Pollard continued. "But obviously it would depend on how much you like your friend. I realize he's an old man, so I wouldn't blame you if you don't think his life is quite as valuable as yours."

Norris.

"What do you think about my offer, Keo?" Pollard asked.

"I don't think very much of it," Keo said.

"Yes, well, it's the best you're going to get these days. Why don't you take a few hours to think about it. Just think fast, though. Time is not on your side. Or Norris's."

"Five?"

"Five," Pollard repeated. "Do we have a deal?"

"I don't know. You sure your boys won't put a bullet in me as soon as I stick my head out there? I just saw two of them shoot a couple of their own in cold blood."

He thought Pollard might have sighed. Maybe the ex-officer had even done it for Keo's benefit. "They're civilians, unfortunately. We've done our best to train them, but as you probably know from your own personal experiences, there are people meant to carry guns, and people who bitch about them loudly on TV. I think we both know which group we belong to, don't we?"

"You don't know anything about me, Pollard."

"Oh, I know plenty. Maybe not all the details, of course, but I know you and I were built for this new world. What were you before the shit hit the fan, Keo? A soldier? A mercenary?"

"Close, but no cigar."

"When I was in military intelligence, I heard stories about private organizations that hired out to the highest bidder. Even the government spooks tread lightly around them. A few of them don't even have names. Some just go by numbers."

"Old wives' tales," Keo said. "Don't believe everything you hear."

"I guess it doesn't matter now. Not anymore. What you were then isn't who you are now. Isn't that right?"

Keo ignored the question and said instead, "Let me think

about your offer."

"You do that," Pollard said. "You have until five to decide. Or until my men find you. Whichever comes first."

"It's awfully reasonable of you and doesn't sound like the maniac who's been stalking me for the last three months at all."

Pollard laughed through the radio. "Five o'clock, Keo. You have until then before I put a bullet in the back of Norris's head."

The radio went silent.

Keo clipped it back to his hip and walked on.

He didn't hear anything else through the radio for the next thirty minutes as he picked his way cautiously through the woods, making as little noise as possible. He stopped every now and then to listen for approaching footsteps. It didn't surprise him that he couldn't hear any more back and forth on the radio. Pollard had recalled his patrols, and they were getting the new frequency in person back at their base right now.

Pollard wasn't a dummy. Far from it. Which meant saving Norris had just gotten much, much harder. Not that it hadn't been before, but now...well, now his chances *really* sucked. At least, if his goal was to save the ex-cop and get out of this alive.

That was, of course, the ideal outcome. A dead man couldn't very well join Gillian at Santa Marie Island, could he?

His watch ticked to 2:25 P.M.

Just a little more than five hours until nightfall, but less than three hours until Pollard ended Norris's existence with a bullet to the back of the head. Keo didn't doubt the man would do just that if he didn't show up at five.

2:26 P.M.

Running out of time...

CHAPTER 10

HE WAITED OVER an hour before the first patrol finally stumbled across him. Keo watched them walking in front of him, oblivious to his presence. He didn't blame them for not noticing. He hadn't moved in over thirty minutes, and he wasn't entirely certain his legs would react the way he wanted them to when the time came.

Fortunately when it was time his body responded just fine, and he pushed himself up with his left arm. His right was gripping the MP5SD, and Keo rose to his knees and took aim from behind the bush.

Two men. Black-clad. Army boots. Assault rifles in front of them.

They had been very quiet, and he wouldn't have heard them coming if they hadn't been walking less than ten meters from where he was lying. He couldn't see their faces, and frankly, he wasn't interested in finding out what they looked like. He had learned long ago that it was easier to kill a man when you didn't bother learning his life story.

He shot the first one in the back of the head, the sound of his gunshot equal to that of a cough, but still loud enough to make a bird above him take flight. There was no echo, which was the point of having a built-in suppressor.

As the man collapsed, Keo swiveled to the right and shot the second one in the throat. He was aiming for the head, but the man was in the process of going into a crouch when he saw his buddy go down. A throat shot was just as good, though, and the man was bleeding and gagging as he sank to his knees.

Keo rushed forward, checking around him for signs of another patrol. When he was sure there wasn't one more in the area, he returned his attention to the two men. One was on the ground on his stomach while the other was on his back, still alive. Both of his hands were wrapped tightly around his throat, trying in vain to stop the blood gushing through his fingers.

He shot the man twice in the chest to put him out of his misery.

The second one had bled all over his clothes, which made him a lost cause. The first one, except for the hole in the back of his head, was for the most part spotless. Keo did his best to ignore the blood trickling out of the man's forehead, where the 9mm round had exited, as he stripped him of his assault vest, then shirt, pants, and boots.

Even as he swapped out his T-shirt and pants for the dead man's clothes, Keo wasn't entirely convinced just looking the part was going to get him any closer to Pollard without being shot on sight. After all, the two in the last patrol had gunned down both Fiona and Rupert anyway, even though they were clearly dressed as one of them. Still, having something that could *potentially* be an advantage was better than nothing. Or, at least, that's what he told himself.

He collected the two dead men's weapons—identical M16s,

neither one with any sort of mounted optic. Which likely made these two part of Pollard's more expendable soldiers. Hell, even Fiona and Rupert had the more mobile and fully-automatic M4s. The M16s were old and clunky and only capable of three-round burst firing.

This is where Norris would grunt and say something like, "If we didn't have bad luck, we wouldn't have any luck at all."

Norris. He had to save Norris. Whatever happened from this moment on, he had to at least try. He owed the old-timer that much.

Keo tossed one of the M16s and slung the other one, then shoved a couple of spare magazines into his pack. Any more and the bag would be too heavy. Right now, he needed mobility and speed.

He grabbed one of the radios and headed off, still moving west toward the shoreline. North would take him right into Pollard's stronghold and likely the bulk of the man's forces. West took him around the shoreline, and if he was lucky, he would be able to circle all the way around and approach the park visitors' building from the rear without being seen.

If being the operative word, of course.

HE THOUGHT ABOUT Gillian, sitting on the beach on Santa Marie Island in the Gulf of Mexico, just off Galveston, Texas. Long black hair glistening under the oppressive southwest heat. Soaking her toes in the cool water and smiling. Bright green eyes looking out at the ocean, waiting for a boat to arrive.

He would be on that boat.

And all he had to do to make that happen was survive today, then find a small enough boat that he could sail with just two people. A sailboat like Mark's, so they wouldn't need to scrounge up fuel for a motor.

Yeah, shouldn't be too hard.

It took him until almost four in the afternoon to circle the park, using the western shoreline as a guide. Having to stay as far away from the roads, the parking lots, and the camping spots as possible contributed to the ticking clock. Robertson Park was ninety-five percent woods and five percent civilization, so it didn't take a lot of effort to stay hidden; it just took a lot of time. That, unfortunately, was something he didn't have in abundance these days, but today in particular.

He knew he was close when he started hearing the roar of ATVs. He went into a crouch beside a large tree as the sound got louder. He didn't have to wait long before three men on all-terrain vehicles appeared across the wide main road, which led into the park and curved its way through the woods.

All three riders were wearing green and black paint over their faces, the barrels of rifles jutting out behind their shoulders. He was surprised to see them riding one-to-a-bike and not doubling up. He wondered what they would do if he stepped out into the road now and picked them off one by one.

But that was a moot point, because the vehicles soon disappeared south down the road, leaving thick, swirling clouds of dust in their wake. They looked as if they were in a hurry and knew where they were going instead of just patrolling. Well, he had left two bodies *somewhere* down in that direction…

He glanced at his watch: 4:15 P.M.

Running out of time…

Keo gave it a minute, waiting for more signs (and noises) of Pollard's men. When he didn't see or hear anything, he got up and raced across the open road. He didn't breathe easier until he had reached the other side and was surrounded by trees and thick bushes again.

He found an empty spot among some underbrush and stopped. Keo pulled out a thin black compact that was already inside the pack when he took it off its dead owner. It looked like something a woman would carry, with a mirror inside and three strips of color—mud brown, green leaf, and flat black. The sweat-resistant camo was durable and would stay on well into the night, though Keo didn't think he would need it in about four more hours.

When he was finished applying the paint to his face, Keo put the compact away, then stood up and continued further into the woods. He walked for another twenty minutes, his progress less productive than he would have liked because he had to stop and hide at every noise he heard or thought he might have heard. He knew he was finally there when he picked up the sound of hammering in the afternoon air.

Keo slowed down, then went back into a crouch behind a thick group of bushes near the edge of a clearing.

So this is what it feels like to walk into the lion's den...

The park visitors' center was really two separate buildings, both L-shaped, with the larger administrative one up front. Driveways led to the front and side doors, and from having stayed in the place previously, Keo knew there were more back doors. Most of the windows had already been boarded up, but a couple of men were hammering 2x4s over the last remaining section of a side window as he arrived.

The parking lot was filled with vehicles, as expected. He counted twelve trucks, but there could have been more parked in other areas he couldn't see. The ones he could see were caked with mud and dirt and showed obvious signs of heavy use. At least four of the vehicles had trailers attached *(for the ATVs)* and were big enough to haul at least four people comfortably, five or six if they felt like squeezing them in.

He counted a dozen or so men standing guard outside, all of them keeping to the main building area. The second building, an old storage warehouse farther in the back, had zero activity around it. Keo paid close attention to the black-clad figures patrolling the roof of the main building with rifles. He spent a second wondering how they had gotten up there, or how they managed not to fall off the sloped rooftop, then decided he didn't care.

Keo had come out of the west side of the park, which gave him a good view of the buildings without being seen himself. The thick rows of bushes in front of him helped, too. He watched now as two ATVs (The same ones he had seen leave earlier? Maybe.) returned, cutting across the parking lot from the south and heading straight to the front twin doors. The entrance was about eighty meters from his position, with two men standing watch outside with AK-47s.

"You have until five to decide. Or until my men find you. Whichever comes first."

He looked down at his watch: 4:46 P.M.

Fourteen minutes until Pollard's deadline.

Keo unslung the M16 and laid it on the ground next to him. Then he went through his pouches and did a thorough inventory of his ammo. He had a feeling he was going to need every single bullet.

4:47 p.m...

WITH EXACTLY FIVE minutes until five, there was a flurry of movement outside the building. Keo didn't have to wait long to find out why.

A tall man strolled outside in black pants, a black shirt, and a black tactical assault vest. The man may have looked like everyone else around him, but there was an obvious difference. It was in the way he moved and in the way he carried himself, even with just a sidearm in a hip holster when everyone else had an assault rifle.

Pollard.

Keo knew who it was even if he had never seen the man before.

Pollard stopped a few meters from the front doors and looked around for a moment before glancing down at his watch—

—*4:56 P.M.*—

—then looking back and motioning toward the entrances.

Norris.

Keo didn't need binoculars to know that the second man stumbling out of the building behind Pollard was Norris.

He was still wearing the same white T-shirt and cargo pants from the day before, and he moved with obvious difficulty, and not just because his hands were bound in front of him. His head hung low, his chin resting against his chest for support as if he had trouble keeping it upright. A third man trailed behind

Norris before catching up to him and grabbing him by the arm. At first Keo thought it was to restrain the ex-cop, but no, it was to keep him upright because Norris couldn't stand on his own.

"Pollard has people with him that know how to get information," Fiona had told him. *"Your friend's in bad shape, Keo."*

Pollard held up his hand, and the man holding Norris upright stopped.

Keo watched as Pollard unclipped his radio, played with the dial, and then held it up to his lips. The radio clipped to Keo's own hip squawked a second later, and Pollard's voice came through. "Keo. It's time."

The radio's volume was turned down on purpose, but it was just loud enough for Keo to hear. He unclipped the radio but didn't respond. He waited instead to see what Pollard would do next.

"Are you there?" Pollard said. "I know you're monitoring the new frequency. We didn't find one of the radios on the two dead bodies you left behind a few hours ago. I had to change the frequency again. Half of my people are confused about which one to use now."

Keo pressed the transmit lever. "How many men do you have left now, Captain?"

"Captain?" Pollard said, sounding amused.

"Major?"

"Close enough."

"Colonel."

"Does it matter?"

"Nah. I was just curious."

"As to your question, I have more than enough," Pollard said.

"I bet I can whittle that number down a little further."

"I'm sure you could with your obvious skills and given enough time. Unfortunately, you're running out of the latter. Or at least, your friend is."

Pollard beckoned with his free hand and Norris was led toward him. Pollard directed them where to go, and Norris was placed in front of the ex-Army officer.

"You're watching this right now, aren't you?" Pollard said through the radio.

Keo didn't answer.

Definitely not a dummy.

Pollard looked around the clearing before expanding his search even further to both sides. The men on the rooftop seemed to catch on and peered down at their surroundings with more purpose. Keo instinctively moved closer to the bush in front of him and prayed that his position, combined with the dark clothes and face paint he had taken off Pollard's people, made him blend in with his surroundings.

"Of course you are," Pollard continued. "Otherwise you wouldn't have bothered answering in the first place. You're not going to let your friend die without trying to do something about it. That's laudable. The problem with that is, whatever you do, it won't be enough."

"All of this just to avenge your son?" Keo said into the radio.

"Why, you think I should do any less for him?"

"Yes, actually."

"You're not a father, or you wouldn't have said that."

"You're right, I'm not a father. But we both know your son had it coming."

Pollard didn't answer right away. Keo saw him looking around and felt a bit of relief because the man was looking in the wrong direction. That relief quickly evaporated when he saw the men gathered in the parking lot starting to spread out, extending outward toward the edge of the clearing.

Two of them were coming in his direction…

"He was still my son," Pollard said. "A life for a life, Keo. I would rather claim yours, but if I need to, I'll take your friend's, too."

"And if I give myself up, you'll let Norris go?"

"You have my word."

"The problem with that is I'm not sure what your word's worth."

"It's worth plenty. But I'm not going to justify myself to you. This has already dragged on long enough. My men are anxious to go back to Corden, and frankly, so am I."

"So go."

"Not until you're dead," Pollard said. Then, "You have one minute to come out of hiding."

Keo measured the distance between himself and Pollard all the way across the clearing a second time.

Eighty meters? Ninety? Give or take.

He looked down at the MP5SD. There was a reason he liked the German weapon. It was mobile and designed for close-quarter combat, and it was damn good at its job. That was the problem. Eighty or ninety meters wasn't a particularly tough shot for a competent shooter armed with a rifle, but he had a submachine gun. Even with the mounted red dot sight, his chances of hitting Pollard from this distance was iffy, and Keo didn't think he was going to get a second shot if he missed the first one.

He slung the weapon and picked up the M16 instead. The American battle rifle was too long, too clumsy, and aesthetically ugly, but it had the Heckler & Koch beat in terms of distance and accuracy. Keo flicked the fire selector to semi-automatic and moved into a shooting position. Eighty meters for the M16 was child's play, even for someone who wasn't trained for sniping.

Like me...

Outside the building, Pollard drew his handgun and pressed it into the back of Norris's head. The ex-cop didn't move. Either he didn't want to give Pollard the satisfaction, or he didn't trust himself to move for fear of falling. God knew Norris could barely stand by himself in the first place.

Keo took a deep breath and settled his right eye over the rear sight of the rifle before letting himself feel the rubber recoil pad at the end of the stock pressed against his shoulder. He eased his hand along the side of the pistol grip before slipping his forefinger into the trigger guard. His off hand wrapped around the fore end before sliding back a bit until he was comfortable with the grip.

He raised the M16 just high enough to shoot over the bush in front of him, but not too high to be noticed by the sentries on the rooftops or *the two guys still walking toward him*. Fortunately for him, they didn't know he was there and were taking their sweet time.

"Keo, you still there?" Pollard said through the radio.

Keo ignored him and sucked in a deep breath instead. He concentrated on remembering all those shooting lessons and tried to ignore the fact that he had never really had to shoot anyone from long distance. That was never part of his job description. His skills involved sterilizing buildings up close and personal, not knocking people off from a football field away.

"Are you still listening, Keo?" Pollard continued. "I'm going to count to ten, then I'm going to execute Norris. He tells me he's an ex-cop from Orlando. That's too bad. I've always been an admirer of law enforcement. It's a tough job."

Keo drew in another deep breath, then expelled it and lowered the sight over Pollard's head. The man was standing with his side facing Keo, which automatically made his head the biggest target. At this distance, it looked like a tiny dot and not the big fat juicy watermelon Keo would have preferred.

"Ten..." Pollard began.

How far had his longest shot been? He couldn't recall, which was the problem. There hadn't been a lot of long shots in his career.

"...nine..."

There was a reason he was so comfortable with the MP5SD and its sound suppressor.

"...eight..."

Eighty meters. Probably more like ninety. Give or take.

"...seven..."

At least there was no wind, just the sweltering heat. So there was that.

"...six..."

It was definitely more like ninety meters.

"...five..."

Or maybe it was more like one hundred meters, for all he knew. Now that was a hell of a shot right there. He was competent, but was he *that* competent?

"…four…"

And all he had were the M16's built-in sights to work with. Jesus, to have something like an ACOG on hand.

"…three…"

Then again, since he was already daydreaming about better optics, why not just go ahead and wish for a bazooka?

"…two…"

That way he could take out Pollard and most of his men at the same time. Of course, that would also mean Norris—

"…one!"

Keo fired.

PART TWO

END OF THE LINE

CHAPTER 11

MAYBE POLLARD HEARD the gunshot and in however many milliseconds it took the 5.56x45mm round to travel eighty meters (or was that ninety?), the ex-military officer managed to move his head just in the nick of time. Or maybe Keo had overestimated his competency with a rifle and his shot was untrue, even with a weapon as sure-shot as the M16.

It could have been either of those reasons, or a hundred other equally viable ones.

The fact was, the outcome was the same: the shot missed and Pollard turned his head and stared right in his direction, and a second later everyone was shooting.

At him.

Keo didn't even know when he decided to do it, but he was suddenly on his feet and racing away from the bushes even as they were shredded by gunfire that seemed to be coming from a hundred different directions all at once. The trees around him didn't stand a chance either, bark flying like arrows, *zip-zip-zipping* at his head and body and legs and arms. Pieces of branches snapped off from above him and rained down like torpedoes.

Keo ran through it all, because stopping meant death.

Somewhere between jumping to his feet and turning, he had discarded the assault rifle and its extra weight. What did it matter? He couldn't shoot worth a damn with the thing anyway, apparently.

About five seconds into his retreat, he managed to somehow tune out the relentless *pop-pop-pop* behind him. After that, it was just the crashing of his breath against his chest, the cold feel of the MP5SD in his hands, the grass slapping against his legs, the *thump-thump-thumping* of his feet against the ground, and the soul-twisting knowledge that he had failed Norris.

I'm sorry, old-timer. I'm so fucking sorry.

Everything was going fine, and he was even picking up speed when there was a sudden sharp pain from his left hip. He might have actually let out a startled gasp, though he couldn't quite be sure with all the sound and fury crashing across his body like ocean waves. When he looked down to the source of the jolt, he saw that the radio was gone, obliterated, leaving behind just the clip still tucked snugly into his belt.

He ran, because if he stopped for even a second to think about anything, he was going to realize that he had just gotten Norris killed because he couldn't make a shot from eighty meters. Hell, a decent grunt could have made that shot. A Boot Camp dropout from the Army would have done better. But not him. *He had missed!*

Now Norris was going to pay the price. Pollard had probably already shot him in the back of the head out of pure spite. Of course, there was a chance Pollard might spare the ex-cop. Or at least realize his value and keep him alive a little while longer, if just to reuse him as bait to lure Keo back out again. It was possible.

Damn, he had almost convinced himself that time.

The shooting had stopped, the branches had ceased exploding, and the ground was no longer kicking dirt in his face. He had blocked out the whole thing so effectively that he didn't even know the air was no longer filled with lead until he slowed down briefly to catch his breath and didn't hear the familiar *pop-pop-pop* anymore.

He pushed himself off the tree and kept moving.

Sorry, old-timer. I screwed up.

You always did say I was going to get you killed, didn't you?

Looks like you were right, after all.

What the hell did he think he was doing, anyway? Even if he had succeeded in putting a bullet through Pollard's brain, it may or may not have even saved Norris's life. At that moment, with time running out, with no other alternative in sight, it had seemed like the right thing to do. If Pollard was dead, maybe the others would let Norris go. Or at least not shoot him. Maybe he could have negotiated with them. But Pollard was in the way, because Pollard ran the show.

If Pollard was dead...

If...*if*...

If squat. You missed.

You missed!

He wasn't tiring yet, but he was getting close. His chest was heaving a little harder than before and his legs were starting to burn. In particular, his right leg. The old bullet wound again? Maybe. His brain could just be making that part up. Probably.

He headed south. Toward the shoreline.

Sorry, Norris. I'm sorry.

He was almost at the road he had crossed earlier when he heard them: *ATVs.*

Keo glanced back as they came up behind him, fast. Two black-clad figures straddling all-terrain vehicles that, at that very moment, looked like predators on wheels. One was yellow, the other white with red stripes. They might have even bared their fangs at him.

I'm losing it. Get a grip!

Keo planted one foot and slid to a stop, spun around, and lifted the MP5SD.

Fifty meters and coming up on him fast. In another second, it was just forty meters. Well within the submachine's effective firing range. Even a weekend wannabe could have made this shot. Which was a good thing now that he knew just what a shitty shooter he was at long distance.

In another second, they were only thirty meters away.

They must not have expected him to stop, because the one on the white ATV jerked on the handles and almost crashed into a tree. Instead, he somehow got his wheels tangled up with some underbrush and the vehicle overturned, sharp edges digging into the ground, the rider holding on for dear life. He should have jumped off the vehicle because it broadsided a tree and flung him off, his hands and legs failing comically in the air as he sailed through open space.

Keo almost laughed at the absurd sight.

The second one must have heard his partner go down because he slowed and looked back, just before Keo shot him twice in the chest. The man flopped off the still-moving ATV, slamming into the ground and rolling forward for a few seconds before stopping in a heap. His vehicle kept going until it crumpled against another tree. Its engines continued running for a moment before finally winding down and shutting off by itself, gasoline leaking into the dirt.

The first man had landed somewhere behind his dead comrade, but he was still alive and picking himself up. He was clearly hurt, but his rifle had somehow remained slung over his back despite the flight and fall. Neither of the two men were wearing helmets, and the one slowly trying to stand up on wobbly legs probably had no idea where he was at the moment.

Always wear a helmet, kids.

Keo almost felt for the guy, though that didn't stop him from shooting the man in the chest anyway. Even before the body had fallen completely to the ground, Keo turned and was running through the woods again.

He kept going, moving, pumping his legs, because if he stopped even for a second, he might start thinking about Norris again.

NORRIS IS DEAD. Keep going.

Gillian is still alive. Get to her.

There's no choice here. One's (probably) dead and the other's (probably) alive.

It was a no-brainer. Norris would understand.

So why was he thinking about how many men Pollard had left? What did the numbers matter if he was retreating, having given Norris up for dead *(if he wasn't dead already)*?

The numbers nagged at him. It always did, even during those days and nights in the insect-infested Louisiana woods, drinking and eating anything they could find while being continually hounded by Pollard's people. He used to wonder if their pursuers ever slept.

So how many were left now? He had killed seven since they cornered him and Norris back at the two-story house. Seven sounded like a lot until you realized how many men Pollard had at his disposal. When you considered that, seven was a miniscule number. Barely worth saying out loud.

Too many left. Always too damn many…

He pushed onward until he could see sunlight filtering through the wall of trees in front of him and smell the fresh water of Downey Creek Lake on the other side. He stumbled into the scalding hot sun against his face and the sand moving under his shoes. It wasn't an impressive looking stretch of beach, but it hid him from the woods and Keo sat down on a fallen log, took out one of Allie's water bottles, and drank it until it was empty.

He closed the bottle back up and put it away. You never knew when an empty container would come in handy. He had learned that the hard way when he and Norris were stuck in the woods and it started to rain, only they didn't have anything to catch it with. They'd had to be content with sticking out their tongues and satiating their thirst that way.

Norris is dead. Forget about him.

Go find Gillian. You promised her.

He tilted his head and soaked in the heat. The warmth was intoxicating. He was content to sit there and bathe in the sun for as long as possible, but the soft *tick-tick-tick* of his watch kept invading his thoughts.

He looked down at it: 5:46 P.M.

Just under two hours until nightfall. He should be looking for shelter right about now, because night was coming.

But then, night was always coming these days, and time always had a way of sneaking by faster and faster, day after day after day…

HE WALKED ALONG the beach for a while, sweating under the sun, and feeling all of two feet tall and fifty pounds after the events of the last hour.

"You're going to get me killed, kid," was one of Norris's constant sayings.

Sorry, old-timer. I guess you were right all along.

Not that the acceptance made the day go any faster. He wasn't even sure what he was doing, or where he was going. The beach went wide at some point, narrow at others. Keo walked along it, wishing he were somewhere else. Like maybe on a different beach, just off the coast of Texas…

He didn't stop until he spotted the long pier extending out of the park about a hundred meters ahead of him. Two figures were moving up the extended wooden frame toward a gazebo at the end overlooking the lake. Another patrol.

Keo went into a crouch and slipped the MP5SD into the ready position.

From his days scouting the park, he remembered an asphalt parking lot behind the pier with a couple of old, abandoned trucks. They both had trailers, because you could launch boats from here. Picnic tables had their own areas, including fire pits, but he couldn't see those from his current position. On the other side of the pier were lakeside homes spread out in their own properties. He had been hoping to find shelter in one of them.

Once the two-man team reached the gazebo, they leaned against the railing and looked around. Neither one had binoculars, so there was little chance they could spot Allie's island somewhere out there in the lake. Even with binoculars, it would have been difficult. That was what made it the perfect spot, after all.

It didn't look as if the men were in any hurry. The shade from the gazebo and the cool breeze coming in from the lake probably had a lot to do with that.

He glanced down at his watch: 6:28 P.M.

He was cutting it too close, taking too big a risk. Even if he found shelter at this point, he would still need to make sure it was empty—of both the human and not-so-human kind. That would probably take another thirty minutes at least.

Running out of time…

But he wasn't getting around those guys. Not without shooting them. And once he did that, the patrol's absence would be noticed and he would have even more of Pollard's goons swarming on his location.

He didn't have a lot of choices.

So what else is new?

Keo got up and turned around to retreat—

He saw them across the distance. Two more men in black moving up the shoreline. They were still far away—about sixty meters—but close enough that as soon as he stood up, they spotted him.

"Hey!" one of them shouted.

Keo darted right, leaping through the trees and back into the woods.

He spent a precious second cursing his bad luck, then put the rest of his energies into running. The problem was, it wasn't just two guys he had to outrun. There were going to be more. Those two back at the pier, too. And how many other patrols were around the area?

Too many. Always too damn many...

He gripped the submachine gun as he ran, prepared for the inevitable firefight that was coming. He didn't know when, he just knew it would be soon. Pollard was right about one thing: Sooner or later he was going to run out of room. Eventually, there would be no more places to hide, no more places to run, and no more places to retreat—

The guy came out from behind the big tree in front of him. He was wearing the same identical black tactical vest as all the others, and the barrel of a rifle poked out from behind one shoulder. But those weren't the things that drew Keo's attention. It was the man's face. Or the white skull, roughly drawn over his face and highlighted with black and green camo paint around the edges.

The hell you supposed to be? ran through Keo's mind just before he saw sunlight glinting off the sharp edge of a knife in the man's hand.

In the split-second that Keo saw the white skull and picked up the flashing knife, he knew it was too late to veer out of the blade's path. He was moving too fast. So Keo threw himself forward and tucked and rolled instead.

Swoosh! as the knife—a Ka-Bar, almost identical to the one he had along his left hip—sliced through the air over his head.

Then he was behind the guy and snapping back up to his feet.

Skull Face was faster, and he was on Keo before he could turn fully around. The MP5SD had managed to come loose from Keo's hands when he did his tuck and roll, and it was now hanging uselessly from his body by the strap. Thank God he hadn't lost it. Without the submachine gun, he only had the .45 Glock—

Stop thinking and move move move!

Keo didn't have time to reach for either weapon because the smiling skull was coming right at him in a blur of steel and black clothes and pearly white teeth. He shoved his hands up and forward on instinct and managed to grab the man's knife hand around the wrist, freezing it in the air. The ambusher looked stunned, as if this was the last thing he had expected, and the smile plastered to his face vanished in the blink of an eye.

Keo lunged forward and drove his right knee into the man's side where the vest didn't protect him and knew he got a part of the ribcage underneath when the guy let out a loud grunt. Keo hooked his leg around the man's and literally swept him off his feet a second later.

Wham!

Skull Face slammed into the ground with another heavy grunt. Keo wrestled the knife out of his hand, then spun it until he had the sharp blade pointing down. The man's eyes widened, the whites merging with the color of the skull. He might have opened his mouth to say something, but Keo didn't give him the chance. He rammed the knife down and into the largest target area—the chest—just an inch over the vest's zipper. The man gagged and groped at Keo's hands, still fighting for possession of the knife with his last breaths.

Keo let him have his knife back and stumbled up to his feet.

He hadn't taken more than two steps when a freight train hit him in the back of the head. His eyes blurred as he lost sight of the woods. But that was the least of his problems. He was falling to his knees without knowing why, the inability to understand filling him with a sense of helplessness that drove him insane. Warm liquid trickled down to the back of his neck and Keo shivered slightly from the contact.

Then he was toppling sideways but somehow managed to twist around so that he slammed into the ground on his back instead of on his stomach. His vision started focusing in on something looming above him.

Aw, Jesus, another one? What is this, Halloween?

Another white skull was hovering over him. This skull looked more orderly, with just black paint along the edges to accentuate the white. Gleaming black eyes, full of mischief, stared down at him. The man was holding an AK-47, and Keo swore he could see his blood (it was surprisingly dark, and were those strings of hair?) on the weapon's buttstock.

Then, the sound of footsteps as someone approached.

"You got him, Jacks?" someone asked.

"Call it in," the man standing over Keo said. For a guy with a white skull painted on his face, Jacks's voice sounded mildly comforting. "Ask the boss what he wants us to do with him."

Then Jacks's face, along with his absurd white skull, started to fade a bit. That may or may not have something to do with why Keo felt as if he were drowning all of a sudden. He found it difficult to concentrate on any one thing because the world kept moving, flickering around like mirages around him.

A muffled (but familiar) voice said, "Bring him back to the base. He's not going to die that easily."

Pollard.

Hands grabbed him and pulled him up from the ground. Someone yanked the MP5SD off him, then someone else ripped the pack and the Glock free. Then they were dragging him through the woods, with Jacks leading the way.

They hadn't been walking for very long when two more figures appeared in front of them like ghosts. One of them also had a white skull painted over his face, but the other one just looked like a normal forty-something who could have been a teacher or a salesman in a previous life.

Skull Face #3 ran past Keo as if he didn't exist. That was fine with Keo. The last thing he needed was another asshole focusing in on him. Everyone else seemed to have just one thing on their minds: Killing him.

A moment later, someone began screaming. It sounded as if he were in pain. Or that could have just been Keo's mind trying to interpret the strange wailing noise. At the moment, he found it difficult to hear much of anything with the ringing in his ears and the warm feel of blood dripping down the back of his neck.

Jacks stopped and turned around, then grinned at Keo. "Man, you just can't stop making friends, can you?"

Keo didn't know how to answer that. He didn't think he could, anyway.

The two guys holding him upright started moving again, passing Jacks, who had stayed behind to watch the show with something that looked like an amused grin on his face.

Keo decided to stop trying to make sense of what was happening around him and let his body go completely slack. If they were going to take him back to Pollard to be killed, he would let them do all the work of carrying him there.

"Who was that?" one of guys dragging him asked.

"Where?" the second one said. "Jacks?"

"No. The other one. The dead guy."

"That's Chris."

"Who's the guy crying over him?"

"Lou. This guy just shanked his brother." The guy went quiet for a moment before adding, "We better tell Pollard. There's no telling what Lou's gonna do to this guy. I've seen him do things..."

"What kind of things?" the other one wanted to know.

"I don't wanna talk about it. Just remember to tell Pollard about what this asshole did to Lou's brother when we get back."

"Jesus," the first guy said. "Was it that bad?"

The second guy didn't answer, though Keo was pretty sure the man had shivered slightly at the question. Unless, of course, he was just imagining it.

CHAPTER 12

"WHAT WAS THAT word? *Daebook?*"

Keo smiled. Or tried to. He couldn't quite focus on the room no matter how hard he tried, much less Norris sitting across from him. "Close enough."

"Didn't your mom ever teach you any other Korean words?"

"Here and there, but Mom embraced being an American wholeheartedly. She liked to say either commit to something, or don't even try. *Daebak* was one of her few exceptions."

"Interesting."

"Is it?"

"Not really," Norris said. "I don't think this is that, huh? There doesn't seem to be anything remotely awesome about this."

"Nope."

"How's the head?"

"Am I still bleeding?"

"Not anymore."

"Then pretty good."

"You look like shit, though."

"Yeah, well, I feel worse."

"I don't see how that's possible."

Keo smirked and sat up on the cold tiled floor. "Thanks for the optimism, old-timer."

They were inside a small back room with an equally small window at the top providing just enough light for Keo to make out Norris's bruised face staring back at him. The room was about five feet wide and ten feet long but felt much more claustrophobic. Norris looked to be in one piece sitting on the floor with his back against the other wall. He wasn't moving, though. Keo couldn't tell if that was because he couldn't, or if he didn't want to.

The former. Definitely the former.

It took him a moment to pick up the empty shelves squeezed into the already small room with them. An old faded yellow mop bucket with a side press wringer was jammed into the corner nearby. There wasn't a lot of room to move without his shoulder hitting something.

The janitorial closet.

From the last time he and Norris had stayed here, Keo knew the room was almost at the end of the main L-shaped administrative building. The front doors would be to his right, with a window facing the side yard to his left. Unless, of course, his memory was fuzzy due to the blow to the head. That was entirely possible, too.

"Glad to see you're still alive," Keo said.

"I guess he thought he might still have some uses for me," Norris said. "I'm not sure about that now that he's got you. Way to go, kid. I thought you'd be smarter than this."

"I guess I got caught up in the whole Murtaugh and Riggs

thing."

Norris grunted. "Now all you need is a faithful dog."

"A dog?"

"Yeah. Riggs had a dog."

"I'm not sure, but I'm reasonably certain dogs are even more endangered these days than us."

"Good point."

Norris was sitting next to a metal door. Through a security glass window near the top, Keo spotted the back of a man's head standing guard outside in the hallway. Light from an LED lamp flooded inside the closet through the small slot under the door.

"How long?" Keo asked.

"About an hour," Norris said. "You got any more bright ideas?"

"Not yet."

"Did you ever have any bright ideas?"

"Nope."

"I figured."

Keo glanced back at the small window above him. The light outside had begun shifting from bright to gloomy.

Night is coming...

He glanced down at his watch, but it was gone. Everything he had was gone, including the black assault vest, gun belt, and of course, his weapons. He saw himself reflected off the metal door across the room. They had even wiped the black and green paint off his face for some reason. At least they hadn't bothered to put him in restraints, so there was that.

Keo touched the back part of his head, where the occasional throbbing was coming from. The sensation was more tingling than full-blown pain. It was still wet back there, but someone had stitched the cut skin while he was unconscious. They had also applied ointment to keep the wound closed. Just feeling the cut made him wince.

"It was just a scratch, relax," Norris said. "The girl that patched you up was also nice enough to clean your face, in case you were wondering."

"Why didn't they just let me bleed to death?"

"Pollard wouldn't let them. He's got plans for you, kid. I don't wanna be you when the sun comes up tomorrow. I mean, it sucks being me now, but the look he gave you?"

"That bad, huh?"

Norris started to say something, but stopped himself. *That bad.*

Keo leaned against the wall, careful to keep his head tilted slightly forward so he didn't bump the wound against the hard concrete. There was a mild dizziness whenever he moved any part of his body too fast, but especially his head.

"What was with the camo and clothes, anyway?" Norris said. "I assumed there was a point to them?"

"I thought it would give me an advantage."

"You didn't really think this through, did you?"

Keo sighed. "I've always been more of a snatch-and-grab kinda guy. Not so much the careful planning. That was always someone else's job."

"I can see that." Then, "You almost had him, though."

"Who?"

"Pollard. That shot—you came close."

"How close?"

"You pissed him off for a good thirty minutes afterward,

that's how close," Norris smiled. "He calmed down after they caught up to you, though. He was a happy little lamb after that. I think he might have even smiled when he thought no one was looking. It was like watching the devil learn to grin for the very time in his life. Gave me the heebie-jeebies."

Now that his eyes had time to adjust to his surroundings, he turned his attention to Norris. The fifty-six-year-old didn't look nearly as bad as Keo had feared. He'd been hit. That was obvious. Keo could see evidence of bruising on his face, jaw, and forehead. But his eyes were in reasonably good shape.

Norris saw how Keo was looking at him and said, "They worked on the body. The face stuff was just to get my attention in the beginning."

"Can you walk?"

"Barely. I think they broke a couple of ribs. I'm not sure. I can't breathe without wishing I was dead."

"*Pollard has people with him that know how to get information. Your friend's in bad shape, Keo.*"

"Sorry, Norris," he said.

"What are you sorry about, kid? I'm the one who got caught."

"How did they catch you?"

"One of their patrols. That girl Fiona wasn't lying. Pollard's got himself a small army out there."

Keo nodded, but didn't know what to say. They stared across at each other for a moment.

"Kid, we've been at this for how long now? Nine, ten months?" Norris said, breaking the silence. "Let's face it, neither one of us expected to survive this long. If it ends tonight, or tomorrow, I'm fine with it. And I'm not pulling that out of my ass. I really am fine with it."

"What about Santa Marie Island?"

"Hey, you're the one with the pretty girl waiting for you. I was never much of a lounging on the beach type to begin with."

Gillian was waiting for him at Santa Marie Island right now, probably wondering what was taking him so long. He imagined her going down to the beach every day to watch the Gulf of Mexico for signs of him.

Sorry, babe, doesn't look like I'll make it there anytime soon.

"Where's Pollard?" Keo asked.

"Probably trying to figure out the most painful way to kill you," Norris chuckled.

"That's not funny."

"I guess it's a matter of perspective. I don't think they're going to be doing anything tonight, though." He glanced at the window above Keo. "You said you're bad with plans?"

"You saw how the last one worked out, didn't you?"

"You better get good at it, then, because I don't think either one of us is going to enjoy what happens tomorrow morning."

"What happened last night?"

"With the bloodsuckers?"

"Yeah."

"They have barricades over the windows and the doors. Takes the ones over the windows down in the day for sunlight, puts them back up at night. They found a key ring the size of my head in one of the offices for all the office doors and they're using it as backup just in case the creatures break through. They haven't yet, though."

"I guess we missed that key ring."

"We didn't have fifty men searching the place, either."

"Looks like they have it all figured out."

"It's a pretty slick operation. You can tell Pollard's had them doing this for a while now. Everyone knows their roles. Hell, if they hadn't been trying to kill me for the last few months, I would have signed up without batting an eye."

"Good to know."

Keo looked up at the darkening window above him. Norris seemed to be doing his best to regulate his breathing, though Keo could hear how labored it was despite the ex-cop's best efforts. Norris was in pain. Even just sitting there, moving almost no part of his body, he was obviously hurting.

"You come up with a plan yet?" Norris asked after a while.

"Not yet."

"Better hurry. For the first time in a long time, night's our friend."

"How you figure that?"

"Pollard and his boys have other things to worry about that don't involve us as long as it's dark outside. That gives you what—ten hours?—to come up with something that won't end up with both of us dead."

"Ten hours?"

"Ten hours."

Keo nodded. "Ten hours, then."

Ten hours to save both our lives.

No pressure.

THEY WERE BOTH alive. For now.

Pollard hadn't bothered to come and talk to him, not even

to gloat a little bit. For some reason, Keo hadn't expected anything less from the man. Even during the chase across the woods there was always a patience, a detached methodology to how Pollard's men pushed them day after day. Or maybe he was just subscribing more to the man than he deserved.

Either way, Pollard had won. He had them dead to rights.

Ten hours to save our lives.

Well, nine, now…

It was pitch black outside, with the only light coming from the hallway outside the door to see by. The guard came and went, and Keo could hear him walking back and forth every few minutes, and sometimes he would appear in the security glass just before moving on again. Apparently standing still had become a chore, and he was doing everything possible to keep himself from getting bored. Or falling asleep. Either/or.

Norris hadn't moved from his spot next to the door. The older man looked tired, his head leaned back, eyes staring up at the dark ceiling as if he could find something interesting up there besides dancing shadows. He looked consistently on the verge of sleep, probably from a combination of fatigue and pain. Keo didn't want to push him on it because Norris clearly didn't want to reveal too much.

The creatures came out as soon as darkness fell. Like clockwork. They were so goddamn predictable.

Keo couldn't see them, but he could feel them. There was something different in the air whenever they were around. A charged atmosphere, fueled by their preternatural existence, the fact that there were hundreds *(thousands)* of them outside at this very moment. He imagined them coming out of the tree lines in swarms from wherever they had been hiding during the day.

Wave after wave of black, pruned flesh and obsidian eyes. Moving silently except for the *tap-tap-tap* of bare feet against the earth.

Keo waited to hear ferocious pounding against the windows and doors, but there wasn't any. That, more than anything, made him uneasy.

"They're up there," Norris said quietly. "On the rooftop. Can you feel them?"

He put both hands on the cold brick wall behind him and stopped breathing for a moment. The vibrations were slight, almost indistinguishable from the normal hum of the night, but if he really focused...

There.

"Yeah," Keo said.

"They were up there last night, too. Running back and forth, probing for weaknesses like they always do. But there aren't any weaknesses. Not last night, and I don't think there's going to be any tonight, either. Pollard's too good, kid. Too thorough. Which translates into a big problem for us. You, specifically."

"What about you?"

"I'm a broken-down old man. You're young and spry, and I get the feeling he's going to want to slice you open to see the insides of the man who killed his one and only offspring."

Keo grinned. "You sure have a way with words, old-timer."

Norris chuckled, but didn't say anything for a while. Finally, he said, "You come up with a plan yet?"

"Nope."

"Are you thinking of one?"

"If it makes you feel better, then sure, I'm thinking of a plan that'll spring the both of us right now."

Norris frowned. "Why are you lying to an old man, kid?"

BY MIDNIGHT, NORRIS had dozed off on the other side of the room. He still hadn't moved from the spot where Keo first saw him when he woke up. Again, Keo guessed it was because he couldn't move, or it hurt too much to try.

Keo had recovered enough to get up and moved around the cramped space. First, he made sure the window was sealed. It was. There was no latch to open it, so nothing was coming through there. Even though it was small—barely 1x1 feet—the bloodsuckers had showed an amazing ability to squeeze into the smallest spaces.

He walked over to the door, and keeping to the side so he couldn't be seen through the security glass, looked out into the hallway. There was a lever, but as Norris had said, the door was locked from the other side. The window was barely a 6x6-inch square at the top of the steel slab, so there was no way he was getting through that.

How the hell was he going to get out before sunup?

He thought there was only one guard, but he was wrong. There were two—a young man in his twenties and an older man in his forties—and they took turns standing outside while the other one walked up and down the hallway.

Keo listened *(hoped)* for sounds of a battle, but there was none. That was disappointing. He couldn't get out of the closet, and by morning Pollard would finally get to do what he had been waiting months for—

Footsteps, approaching from the right side of the hallway. This one was different. It was loud, made by someone moving with purpose.

"What are you doing here?" the younger guard outside the door asked, looking up the hallway at the source of the heavy footsteps. "You're not supposed to be down here."

A second voice answered, but Keo couldn't make out the words. It didn't sound as if they were having an argument, though.

"You shouldn't be here," the guard said again. He didn't sound angry, but more confused and a bit indecisive.

"Where's Willie?" the newcomer said. He was close enough now that Keo could hear him if he pressed his ear against the door.

"He went for a bathroom break," the guard said. "You didn't see him?"

"I must have passed him by. I need a favor, Barry."

Barry, the guard, shook his head. "You know I can't help you, Lou. I have orders. You're not supposed to go anywhere near him. Pollard said—"

There was a flurry of movement—too fast for Keo to catch in time through the small opening—as something seemed to hit Barry in the throat. A hand. A very fast-moving hand. The guard gagged and grabbed at his neck, just as something else hit him in the face (this time Keo saw it pretty clearly—it was the stock of a rifle) and Barry dropped beyond his field of vision.

"Stay down," the man named Lou said. "Willie's fine; he's just taking a nap in the bathroom. You'll be, too, as long as you stay out of my way."

Keo stood up on his tiptoes and peered down at Barry,

crumpled on the floor next to the door, as Lou knelt down and rifled through his pockets. Barry was still alive, but his face had turned blue as he struggled to breathe.

Lou found what he was looking for—a key—and stood up. He turned around and looked into the security glass at Keo. Late thirties, red beard, and hard brown eyes pierced the peephole. He had an AK-47 slung over his back, and there were still remnants of white paint on his face where a skull used to be before he had washed it off.

"Lou," one of the men who had dragged Keo through the woods earlier had said. *"This guy just shanked his brother. We better tell Pollard. There's no telling what Lou's gonna do to this guy. I've seen him do things..."*

Keo took a step back as Lou unlocked the door and pushed it open. He stood in the bright hallway, one hand on the butt of his sidearm, and didn't make any further move to enter the room. He was shorter than Keo, but he made up for it with broad shoulders and muscle. The guy outweighed him by fifty pounds easily.

"You don't know me, do you?" Lou asked.

Sure I do, I shoved a knife into your little brother's chest, Keo thought, but he figured he needed to stall for time, so he said instead, "No."

"Lou," the man said.

"What's this about, Lou?"

"I had a brother. Chris. You remember him, don't you?"

"I don't know any Chris."

Stall for time.

And then what?

Good question...

Lou took his hand away from his sidearm and pulled a sheathed Ka-Bar knife from behind his back. He pulled the blade out, the hallway light glinting off the sharp edge. "You recognize this?"

Keo did, but he shook his head anyway. "A knife's a knife. What about it?"

"It's my brother's. It belonged to Chris. You killed him with it this afternoon. You remember now?"

Keo stared back at Lou, saw the pain, anger, and hatred glaring back at him. He looked past Lou at Barry, lying on the floor, the LED lamp hanging from a hook nailed into the wall. Poor Barry was either dead or unconscious, because he wasn't moving at all. His face was covered in blood that had drooled out of his shattered nose.

Keo's eyes shifted back to Lou. "So what is this, revenge?"

"Yeah," Lou said. He tossed the sheath to the floor and tightened his grip on the knife. "That's exactly what this is."

"You took out both of my guards just to get to me? I'm flattered. But I'm not sure Pollard's going to be very happy with you. From what I hear, he can be a real hard ass when people disappoint him."

"I don't give a shit what Pollard says," Lou said, spitting out the words.

Oh, I can see that. You clearly don't give a shit anymore, my friend.

"Why should he be the only one who gets his pound of flesh?" Lou said. He clutched and unclutched the knife handle. "I'm going to make you scream, and no one's going to stop me."

Keo's eyes fixed on the open door behind Lou.

There. That was his way out.

Literally, in this case.

Who says I can't come up with a plan?

Oh right, everyone.

"Do you even remember him?" Lou asked. "Do you even *remember?*"

"Of course I remember," Keo said, and stared right back at Lou. "He was a little bitch, your brother. He started crying when I punched that knife through his chest—"

Lou lunged, the Ka-Bar slashing, his face locked in a half-scream.

CHAPTER 13

THE KA-BAR KNIFE had a seven-inch straight-edge blade with a five-inch brown leather handle. It weighed just barely half a pound and had a serrated section near the guard for tough cutting. It was a sharp and highly effective fighting knife, and it was the reason Keo had been carrying one around ever since he had picked it up from Earl's basement. This one wasn't Keo's—his had a black handle—but it sure as hell looked just as capable of eviscerating him.

He jumped back and twisted sideways as Lou struck, shooting the knife forward at him. Lou moved with surprising swiftness for a guy carrying his bulk, and Keo was preparing himself for the follow-up attack as soon as the knife missed its mark. Even so, he wasn't quite ready when Lou threw a shoulder into his chest, knocking him into the empty shelf along the wall.

Lou was operating on what Keo called Primal Mode. He was out of control and nowhere close to thinking about his next move before doing it. He was letting his emotions dictate his every action, and that made him predictable. All Keo had to do was let the man do all the hard work and overexert himself.

When the first strike didn't connect, Lou tried again, cutting from right to left this time (a predictable move, because it was also the most obvious choice), the arc of the knife slashing from waist-level to shoulder blade. Keo spun out of the way easily and the Ka-Bar *clanged!* against the metal shelves, throwing sparks into the darkened room for just a split-second. Keo wondered if anyone outside the closet had heard that. The last thing he wanted was Pollard's people to rush down the hallway and stop this.

Okay, time to finish this.

Before Lou could bring his arm back for a third try, Keo grabbed it at the wrist and pinned the knife hand against the shelf. He slammed the palm of his left hand into Lou's right arm, just below the elbow, and heard the satisfying *crack!* of Lou's arm breaking at the elbow joint.

Lou's scream vibrated through the entire building.

Oh, great. Everyone definitely heard that.

Keo silenced Lou by wrapping the fingers of his right hand around the man's wrist, pulling it back, then twisting the lifeless broken arm backward. Lou knew what Keo was trying to do and attempted to let go of the knife, but Keo wouldn't let him. He tightened Lou's fingers around the handle and guided the point of the Ka-Bar into Lou's chest. It was, he thought, about the same spot where he had also killed Lou's brother earlier in the woods…and with the same knife, too.

Lou's legs gave out and he collapsed to the floor, Keo hanging over him until the very last second, when he finally let go of the sagging body.

"Sorry about your brother," Keo said.

Lou gasped up at him like a fish on dry land. His useless

right arm lay helplessly at his side while he groped at the knife handle with his left, trying in vain to pull it out. Either he didn't have the strength or he had forgotten how to do something as simple as pull.

Keo stopped paying attention to the dying Lou. He could hear footsteps almost right away, pounding down the hallway along with someone screaming orders.

"I need your gun," Keo said.

He grabbed Lou and turned him over onto his side and pulled the AK-47 off him. Lou might have made a noise, but Keo wasn't listening to him anymore. He focused on the world outside the door as he fumbled with the assault vest and pulled out two spare magazines and stuffed them into his pockets.

He looked up just in time to see Norris opening his eyes and staring back at him. "So this is your plan?"

Keo grinned. "Stay put."

"He dead?" His eyes were on Lou's gasping form.

"Soon."

"Okay," Norris said, and closed his eyes and seemed to fall back to sleep.

Keo flicked the fire selector on the AK-47 to full-auto and stepped over Lou's body and headed for the door. He stuck his head out and looked left, saw the window at the end about two meters away, right where he expected it to be. It was barricaded with pieces of lumber that covered up the entire frame, and a large metal filing cabinet was laid over the whole thing as additional reinforcement. Keo couldn't see a single stream of moonlight penetrating the makeshift shield.

Turning right was a different story: Three men with rifles were rushing down the hallway at full speed. They looked like ghosts moving among the shadows that dominated the passageway, running in and out of a pair of LED lights hanging in their path.

He stepped outside, legs on either side of Barry's prone form, and opened fire on them. He dropped two with the first pull. The third somehow managed to duck the volley, turned, and started running back in the direction he had come.

Keo fired another burst and knocked the man off his feet just as he was about to reach the turn. He spilled to the floor and actually slid along it for a few feet before coming to rest.

Yeah, everyone definitely heard that, too.

He turned and ran straight for the barricaded window. He grabbed the metal cabinet and pulled it loose from the wall, then stepped quickly aside as it toppled. Keo was already smashing the stock of the AK-47 against the wooden slabs even before the cabinet hit the floor, spilling drawers with the kind of racket that could be heard from every part of the building.

Thwack-thwack-thwack!

The AK-47 was easily one of the world's most durable weapons ever invented by man. Originally put into production by the Soviets in 1949, it continued to be employed with great effectiveness on battlefields around the world six decades later. There wasn't a part of the planet Keo had done work in that didn't have piles of the rifle. It was both amazing and a bane of his existence.

The one Keo was wielding now had a wooden buttstock with a steel butt plate, and as he rammed it repeatedly against what looked like a repurposed countertop, he could feel the weapon disintegrating in his hands. But even as the assault rifle slowly chipped, it was cratering his target, until—

Thwack!

The first board broke in half, and Keo saw a pair of dark black eyes peering in at him through the opening. There was no glass on the other side because it had been broken months ago. The creature reached in almost as soon as the small section of makeshift wall collapsed under the pounding from the AK-47.

Keo moved over to his left and started working on another piece of countertop, even as hands—one, two, *three*—fumbled and grabbed and tried to punch and pull and push their way through the opening. Keo ignored them—not an easy feat, because they were right in front of him and he could *smell* them—and kept flailing at the next piece of the barricade.

Thwack-thwack-thwack!

He did his best to ignore the stench, the fact that there could very well be hundreds of the monsters outside the window at this very moment, seeing him, trying to claw their way in to get at him, their frenzied state heightened beyond belief—

Thwack!

A second board broke a split-second before a loud *crack!* exploded across the hallway and a bullet smashed into the wall an inch to the left of his head.

Keo dropped to the floor and spun around just as four figures rushed up the flickering darkness. They were already halfway to his position and were aiming when Keo threw himself forward and slid along the smooth tiled floor. His momentum carried him all the way to the open janitor's closet door, where he grabbed the doorframe and pulled himself inside, just barely avoiding sliding into Barry's unmoving body.

He twisted onto his back—which was faster than getting

up—and slid against the opening. Instead of paying attention to the men approaching him from his right, he looked left and opened fire on the window.

He wasn't aiming at the gaping hole he had created earlier, or at the dozens of skeletal black arms trying to tear their way inside—or the ocean of quivering black flesh already visible in the center—but at the pieces of the barricade still in place. He fired on full-auto, pouring everything left in the magazine into the same general area.

Behind him, he glimpsed the men slowing down before stopping completely and going into a crouch against the walls. One had flopped to the floor on his stomach. He guessed they had no idea what he was doing, but was reluctant to keep coming when they could see he was armed and shooting.

When he was empty, he shoved in a new magazine and immediately started firing again. He concentrated this new group of rounds on different sections, weakening the boards one at a time. Then one of the creatures managed to push a large slab free and it tumbled to the floor, and now two of them were pushing their heads through the newly formed opening, just big enough for a full-size bloodsucker to come through.

The first creature dropped through the hole and *plopped* on the hallway floor. Another one was already squeezing through behind it, even as another bullet-riddled slab of wood was forced free from the wall.

Gunfire clattered from nearby and bullets smashed into the creatures. Five of them found their mark against the first bloodsucker that had managed to fall through the opening, and the undead thing jerked as rounds slammed into it. There was a *ping!* as a bullet ricocheted off bone and smacked into a nearby wall.

Not that it did any good in stopping the tide. They were coming through the window, pushing against the remaining barricade. And each time one of them made it inside, bullets poured into it, some punching through their weak flesh and hitting the wood or wall behind them.

Two were inside now.

Then three.

Then four—

Ten—

Keo grabbed the lever above him and swung the door shut. It closed with a loud *bang!* just as the first creature slammed into it from the other side. The lever in his hand quivered as the bloodsucker attempted to push it open, but he was stronger. He couldn't lock it from this side, so Keo hung on for dear life instead. Thank God dying *(re-dying?)* hadn't given them any extra strength, or else he would be screwed right about now.

He ignored the balled black fists that began whaling on the security glass above his head. The window cracked, but the noise was quickly drowned out by the overwhelming gunfire exploding up and down the hallway outside.

Then the entire length of the building shook violently under the noise and fury as the black-eyed monsters began rushing past the closet door. He could hear them, the *tap-tap-tap* of their bare feet against the tiled floor like a stampeding herd.

Keo kept his head down and watched the pool of LED light shining under the door flickering wildly as the bloodsuckers ran across. Then slowly, inch by inch, the light faded. No, not faded. It was simply being overwhelmed by the number of creatures right outside his door at this very second.

Moments later, the screaming started…

LOU DIED WHILE Keo was outside trying to open up the window so the creatures could flood the building. The dead man lay perfectly still in a small pool of blood, the Ka-Bar still embedded in his chest.

"Live by the Ka-Bar, die by the Ka-Bar."

Wasn't that the old saying?

Close enough.

Random thoughts like that kept Keo from hearing the screaming beyond the janitor's closet door. The creatures had stopped trying to get at him through the small security glass window. One or two had sliced themselves on the remaining shards, but the opening was too narrow for anything bigger than an arm. After a while they stopped trying, especially when there was other, easier prey elsewhere.

The screams and gunfire went on, nonstop, for nearly two hours. Keo didn't know how Pollard's men could keep up the pace for so long. Eventually, everything seemed to come to a grinding halt, and there was only the occasional gunshot. For him it seemed to have taken less than half an hour, but he imagined it must have felt like an eternity for the people going through it.

He could hear them still moving in the hallway. The LED lamp was gone, either turned off *(unlikely)* or broken during the initial surge. But there was still moonlight shining through the small window behind him, enough for Keo to see the puddles of blood that had leaked into the room through the slit under the door. Maybe some of that even came from Barry, the guard that Lou had incapacitated earlier.

Keo hung onto the door lever all night, shifting his position every ten minutes to keep from becoming complacent. They hadn't tried to force their way in since the first hour of the invasion, but every now and then he felt the lever moving slightly.

Probing. They're always probing…

Sometime around midnight (at least according to his internal clock), Keo stood up and sneaked a peek through the broken security glass and at the hallway outside. He did it tentatively, fully expecting one of the creatures to pop up and give him a good scare like in the movies. What were the rules of surviving a horror flick?

"Don't go into the basement!"

"Don't split up!"

"Don't look out into the hallway full of bloodsucking creatures!"

He looked through the 1x1 square hole. It took his eyes a moment to adjust to the semidarkness on the other side. If not for the moonlight pouring in through the now-open window, he wouldn't have been able to see the bloody footprints that covered the floor, so many that it was impossible to tell the tiled lines apart from the deformed footprints.

He could hear them moving around outside the door—*sense* them—but he couldn't actually see them. They were concentrated further up the hallway to his right, where the bulk of Pollard's people were gathered for the night. Where the offices were.

How many were still alive, hiding inside those rooms right now? One? Two? A dozen? Maybe none. Had Pollard himself made it?

How many more hours left? Six, give or take, before dawn?

"It's always bloodiest before the dawn."

Wasn't that the old saying?

Close enough.

"WE'RE ALIVE," Norris said, opening his eyes.

"You sound surprised," Keo said. "I told you I'd get us out of here."

"How the hell are we still alive?"

"Because I'm good."

"Good, or just really lucky?"

Keo grinned. "Same difference. Bottom line is, we're still alive."

Norris's eyes went from Lou's body to the window on the back wall. He turned his head—or turned as much of it as he could, anyway—to look at the door Keo was leaning against, hands gripping the lever as if his life depended on it because, well, it did.

"I can hear them outside," Norris said.

"That's impressive. I'd have thought hearing was the first thing to go with old age."

Norris grunted. "Wiseass."

"Three hours," Keo said.

"Three hours?"

"Until dawn. Three more hours until we need to get the hell out of here."

"What about Pollard?"

"I don't know. He might be dead or alive, or hiding some-where. The shooting stopped hours ago."

"Pollard's too mean to die. You need to be careful."

"You mean *we*, don't you, old-timer?"

"No." Norris sighed. "Remember when you asked me if I could move?"

"Yeah…"

"I lied. I can't move."

"I figured that."

"I mean it, kid. I can't even lift my arms." He attempted to raise both arms, but his hands barely left the floor before he gave up. "I'm done. When the sun comes up, you need to get the hell out of here before Pollard's people poke their heads out from wherever they're hiding right now. That's your only shot unless you plan to take on however many of his people are still left. Could be a few or a lot. Don't take that chance."

Keo stared at Norris for a moment. The older man's eyes were on Lou, either because he found the dead body fascinat-ing, or (more likely) he didn't want to look Keo in the eyes.

"Are you telling me to leave you here?" Keo finally said.

"I'm telling you I'm no good out there. It is what it is. Look, I'm fifty-seven—"

"I thought you were fifty-six?"

"My birthday was a month ago."

"Why didn't you say anything? Happy birthday."

Norris smirked. "Thanks. Anyway, as I was saying…"

"I'm not leaving you here, old-timer."

"The hell you're not." He finally met Keo's eyes over the very short distance. "Santa Marie Island. Remember? Gillian? Jordan? The others? You made a promise, kid. It's your job to keep it."

Keo didn't answer him.

Norris smiled. "She'd kick my ass if she knew you were tossing your life away for someone who couldn't even walk. I don't need that little girl all up in my grill, kid. She can be pretty mean when she's angry."

Keo looked through the broken security glass. It was dark outside, but he could see their shapes moving about. As if on cue, the lever moved against his hand. It was very slight, almost tentative.

More probing...

"They're out there?" Norris said.

Keo nodded. "They can hear us talking. It's so quiet, they'd be able to hear from outside the building."

"Remember, at sunrise, you need to get gone."

Keo didn't say anything.

"Kid," Norris said. "You heard me?"

"Yeah, I heard you."

"Head south. Find a map and a car and get down to New Orleans. Find a boat and get to Galveston. You promised her."

Keo didn't say anything.

"Kid," Norris pressed.

"Yeah," Keo said.

"Sunrise. In three hours. Got it?"

Keo nodded. "I got it."

"Good," Norris said, leaning his head back and closing his eyes.

Keo kept his focus on the hallway outside. Thinking. Trying not to think. But unable to stop himself.

Norris had a point. The chances of Pollard's entire fifty-something men roster succumbing to the creatures in one fell swoop was too much of a best-case scenario to even bother hoping for. There would be survivors.

How many? That was the question.

He didn't have a watch, but he could feel the encroaching dawn.

Two hours.

Two more hours until I abandon Norris to die in a stinking closet.

CHAPTER 14

AT LEAST LOU had had the decency to come try to kill him with a full tactical belt. Keo stripped the dead man of it now, including side holster and ammo pouches. He pulled the Ka-Bar knife out of Lou's chest and put it back into its sheath, then attached it to the belt on his left hip. The sidearm was a Sig Sauer 1911 .45 semi-automatic, and he still had the AK-47. The assault rifle's buttstock was cracked, but everything else was fine when he dry fired it to make sure. He was down to just one magazine, which was the problem.

There were no signs of Pollard's people outside the hallway, dead or otherwise, so there was no scavenging for more weapons and ammo. He spent a second or two thinking about where the bodies went, if the creatures took them, and let it go just as quickly. It didn't matter.

Instead, he concentrated on what did: Getting the hell out of the building without having to fight his way through however many of Pollard's people remained.

How much time was left?

It wasn't long now. He could feel the heat starting to fill up the hallway outside, the pool of light gradually creeping along the *(bloodied)* floor an inch at a time. The creatures, clearly sensing the coming morning, had left close to an hour ago. The sudden rush of bare feet slapping against blood-slicked tiles was a startling and wholly unique sound Keo wasn't sure he wanted to hear ever again.

He waited patiently, watching as a small swath of light began to grow...

Now or never.

He threw the door open and stepped outside, swinging the rifle left, then right. He ignored the congealed pool of blood under his shoes, the *plop-plop* that filled the air with every movement he made.

The hallway was empty, and there was enough sun coming through the open window behind him that he could see the still-dark wall of trees across the side yard. It wasn't completely light outside, but there was enough that birds had begun to chirp in the background.

Take your cues from the furry creatures in the trees. What could possibly go wrong?

Keo looked right again, just to be sure, before hurrying back into the closet.

Norris's eyes were closed. They had been closed for the last couple of hours since their last conversation. Keo crouched next to him and felt his pulse. He wasn't sure if he could even see the older man breathing under his shirt.

There.

It wasn't much, but it was there. Norris was still alive, if barely.

"Old-timer," Keo said.

Norris didn't respond. His breathing remained shallow,

labored, and his eyelids didn't seem to be moving at all.

"Norris."

Still nothing.

Keo tapped the ex-cop lightly on the cheek. When that didn't work, he tapped harder.

"Norris. Wake up."

Zero reaction.

Keo glanced up and out the security window and could see light beginning to spread along the ceiling in the hallway.

Time's up.

He smacked Norris so hard he was sure he had rattled a tooth or two.

Norris's eyes flew open and he glared at Keo. "Jesus, you're still here."

"We gotta go."

"Go where?"

"Anywhere but here."

Norris shook his head. "I told you, kid, I can't move, much less walk—"

"Then I'll drag you. I got at least fifty pounds on you. Most of that is muscle. You're what, 150 of old man bones and wrinkled skin?"

Norris grunted. "You little shit."

Keo grinned. He opened the door and peered out again, looked left then right, before sitting for a moment just to listen. He couldn't hear anything; just the birds outside the window. The entire building was dead quiet. Amazingly so. The pool of light had only reached a few feet beyond the closet door. Most of the hallway to his right was still covered in thick patches of darkness, with the turn at the very end indistinguishable.

He slung the AK-47 and positioned Norris away from the wall. "I'm going to be dragging you through blood and God knows what until we get to the window."

"Just go, kid."

"Shut up and play dead. Not literally, of course."

Norris sighed but didn't argue.

Keo wrapped his arms around the older man's shoulders, heard him grunt with pain, then began dragging him to the door. He was grateful for the smooth tiled floor (covered in blood or not), otherwise the bruises under his clothes would be the last thing Norris had to worry about. Even so, it was like dragging a heavy bag of flour, albeit one that was just barely breathing.

In the hallway, he turned left and dragged Norris backward toward the window.

"Jesus," Norris said. "Whose blood am I sliding around in?"

"I think it's one of the guards. Barry something."

"One guy?"

"Sure, let's go with that."

"Oh Jesus, kid, this ain't right."

The blood was everywhere, on the floor and along the walls. Just the red variety, because the tainted black kind, Keo knew, evaporated against sunlight. He could still smell some of it lingering in the air, like stinging acid.

There were dried, bloody prints along the walls and ceiling, which he didn't know was possible. How the hell did they get up there? Were they running on each other's heads? He would have dismissed that as the ramblings of a crazy person, but he had come to realize there were very few things the creatures were not capable of when they sensed prey. And last night there had been plenty of humans inside the building.

It must have been a feeding frenzy. Sucks to be them.

It didn't take long to reach the window. There were no glass shards along the frames for him to worry about because all the windows along the building had been broken out months ago. There were just the repurposed countertops, most of them perforated by the two AK-47 magazines he had sent their way last night. There were only a few boards still hanging from nails along the walls, and it didn't take much to slide them out of the way.

"You ready?" Keo asked.

"No," Norris said.

"You're gonna have to do most of the work here. Or I can just throw you out—"

Norris pushed his way onto his feet before Keo could finish. He turned around, Keo holding him up the entire time. He led Norris toward the window, feeling like a parent guiding a big and lumbering toddler.

"This is goddamn embarrassing, kid," Norris grunted.

"Out you go," Keo said.

"Wait—"

Keo didn't wait. He pushed Norris through the wide opening, something that hadn't been there last night. Norris disappeared through the hole and landed on the other side with a *crunch!*

Keo hoped he hadn't landed on the back of his neck.

"Oh, you little asshole," Norris said from the other side of the window.

I guess not.

He hurried out after giving the long (and dark, but brightening up fast) hallway another look. He went through the window feet first, landing on the other side next to Norris, who had managed to sit up on the ground, supporting himself with both elbows.

"You in one piece?" Keo asked.

"No thanks to you."

"Can you shoot?"

"I need to?"

"Maybe."

"Then I guess I can."

Keo drew the Sig Sauer and handed it to Norris before helping him up and wrapping one arm around his waist. He hooked Norris's left hand around the back of his neck, which left the ex-cop with his right hand free to hold the gun.

"Try not to shoot me in the leg," Keo said.

"It's tempting," Norris said.

It felt like Norris had gained an additional fifty pounds since Keo dragged him out of the janitor's closet. Of course, now he was shouldering the man's entire weight instead of just pulling him around like a useless sack of meat, so that might have had a little something to do with it, too.

"Where we going?" Norris asked.

"Anywhere but here."

He glanced back at the broken window and into the pitch-black hallway at the far end one last time, then began moving the two of them away from the building. Norris walked as much as he could, but Keo could tell it was taking a lot out of him even just to shuffle his feet one step at a time. It took Keo a few seconds to adjust to Norris's non-existent pace.

"You sure it's safe in there?" Norris said, staring at the dark woods in front of them. "I can't see shit."

Keo blinked at the rising sun, comforted by the warmth massaging his face. It wouldn't be completely light for another five, maybe ten minutes. But there was enough to get by, or at least send the creatures back to their hiding places. For once, the bloodsuckers' seemingly innate ability to sense the coming dawn, that allowed them to rush off well in advance of the sunlight, would work in their favor.

Unless, of course, he was wrong about the whole thing.

"There's plenty of light," Keo said. "We'll be fine."

HE WAS HOPING for an hour, but realistically only expecting thirty minutes. It turned out to be more like twenty before he heard the first burst of engines coming from behind them. It would have been nice if he had grabbed one of those. Of course, that would mean finding the key or hot-wiring one. Could you even hot-wire an all-terrain vehicle?

It would also have been nice if Norris could move a little faster, too. As much as he was pushing the old-timer, they made slow progress.

"Aw, dammit," Norris grunted, when he heard the engines start up behind them. "You gotta go on, kid. I'm just slowing you down."

"Shut up and keep moving," Keo said.

"This is it for me. The faster you accept that, the better chance one of us will live through this."

"You talk too much. Keep moving."

"Kid—"

"Which part of shut up and keep moving don't you understand?"

Norris sighed. "You damn whippersnappers. You never listen."

They had only managed to put about a hundred meters between them and the clearing when Keo heard not one, but at least three, ATVs revving their engines. So that meant at least three survivors from last night's attack. More, if they decided to ride piggyback. How many of the sports vehicles had he seen? A dozen?

Too many. Always too damn many...

"We gotta pick it up," Keo said.

"I would if I could," Norris grunted back. "I told you, just leave me here. I got a gun. I'll try to give you some extra time."

Keo said nothing.

"Kid," Norris said.

"Shut up and walk faster."

"What is this, a death wish? You did everything you could. You even came back for me, for God's sake. I didn't expect that, but you did, and I'm grateful—"

Crunch-crunch.

Keo didn't so much as drop Norris as he simply cast him off to one side. Even as he was spinning toward the source of the sound, he was unslinging the AK-47 from his shoulder, praying that dry firing the weapon back earlier had been enough to make sure it was still in one piece and would work when he needed it, like now.

"Aw, geez," Norris said as he landed on the ground with a *thump.*

Keo didn't have time to make sure he was all right. He was

already peering through the assault rifle's iron sight at a large bush standing up next to a tree. It looked as if a part of the woods had come alive and were staring back at him.

Wait. *Staring* back at him?

"Goddammit, Zachary," Keo said, lowering the rifle. "I almost shot you."

Zachary grinned, white teeth showing behind the layer of dirt and mud that covered his face. He walked toward them in his ghillie suit. "You look like shit."

"You smell like it too, San Diego," a second voice said behind him.

Keo looked over at Shorty, wearing his own ghillie suit, emerging out from behind a tree. Both men looked as if they had slept in the woods all night.

And Norris thinks I'm *crazy.*

"Holy shit, I think I'm losing my mind, kid," Norris said, somehow managing to sit up on the ground, "because I think the forest is coming alive and talking to me."

Keo smiled. "Don't shoot. They're friends."

"Shoot? I can't even lift my hands. I told you that." Both of Norris's arms were flat on the ground beside him, including the one holding the Sig Sauer.

"I guess you found him, huh?" Zachary said.

"Yeah," Keo said. "What are you guys doing here?"

"Shorty and I were bored on the island, so we decided to come watch you get yourself killed."

"Island?" Norris said.

"Long story," Keo said. "Can you guys give me a hand with him?"

"Depends," Zachary said. "Can he do anything other than

look mostly dead?"

Norris grunted. "I'm way too old for this shit."

WITH ZACHARY AND Shorty's help, they were able to cover more ground. The two men were racing through the woods, carrying Norris between them. Norris's body had gone slack, though Keo couldn't tell if he was just tired or unconscious. Keo trailed behind them, keeping his ears and eyes open. In less than five minutes, they had gone nearly 200 meters, five times the distance he and Norris had managed in the previous twenty minutes by themselves.

The continued roar of the ATVs had changed behind them, and Keo knew the vehicles were now moving.

He stopped, but Zachary and Shorty didn't. The older of the two men threw a look over his shoulder and met Keo's eyes.

"Go, I'll catch up," Keo said.

"Same place as last time," Zachary said. "We'll wait thirty minutes. If you're not there by then—"

"Thirty minutes. Go."

Zachary narrowed his eyes at him. Keo guessed the older man already knew what he was planning. "You're insane, you know that?"

"Look who's talking. The guy who slept last night in the woods voluntarily."

Zachary grinned. "Good point. I'll see you when I see you."

"Don't wait for me."

Zachary nodded, turned, and continued forward.

"Adios, San Diego!" Shorty shouted, just a bit too loudly.

The sight of them vanishing between two huge trees was surreal. Shorty and Zachary, in their ghillie suits, looked like monsters hauling off an unconscious victim. If he were a child, it might have given him nightmares.

Keo slid behind a tree and faced back toward the park visitors' building before taking inventory of what he had left.

There was the Sig Sauer .45 he had taken back from Norris. It still had eight rounds. The AK-47 was still loaded with the full magazine, which was thirty more.

Thirty-eight bullets.

I've had to make do with less.

HE WAITED AND listened. It sounded as if the vehicles were spreading out, going in different directions, trying to cover as much ground as possible.

He was trying to figure out if that was a good thing or a bad thing. The point here was to draw the chase *to* him and away from Shorty and Zachary. But if the pursuers were spreading out, he wouldn't be able to effectively do that—

The man burst through the bushes on a beat-up yellow Yamaha, turning all the scenarios in his head into a moot point.

The all-terrain vehicle was chewing up the ground at a fast clip—probably moving a little too fast for someone traveling in a world full of unmovable objects that could end his ride at any second with the slightest wrong turn. The man didn't seem to notice the potential dangers, though, and Keo was glad to see he was alone.

The vehicle was twenty meters away when Keo spun out

from behind the tree and into the oncoming vehicle's path. He was close enough—and getting closer with every second—to see the rider's widening eyes.

He fired off a burst, shattering one of the front headlights. Pieces of the brake lever exploded and filled the air. A split-second later the rider flipped backward off the seat, which kept going long after it had lost its rider. Keo cursed and ran out of the vehicle's path as metal and plastic and chrome flashed by him in a blur, two inches or so from clipping him as it continued going on its own before smashing into a tree and coming to rest.

Keo stumbled back up to his feet and rushed forward.

The man was still alive, though his legs looked like pretzels under his awkwardly positioned body. One hand was clutching his stomach, where blood squirted out between his fingers, while the other was reaching for his weapon, which had fallen during his tumble and now lay a few feet from his outstretched hand.

Keo smiled at the sight of the Heckler & Koch MP5SD on the ground. He picked it up and gave the familiar dents and scratches a quick brush with his fingers. He didn't think he'd see it again, so it had to be fate that the submachine gun would, literally, fall back into his lap.

Fucking daebak.

He crouched next to the rider, ignored the man's pleading eyes, and opened his pouches and pulled out three long magazines and two shorter ones for the 9mm Glock that Keo also pulled out of a holster. The man grimaced silently through the pain, pale blue eyes watching Keo with a measure of anticipation and hate.

"Is Pollard alive?" Keo asked him.

The man stared at him, but didn't answer.

"How many of you are still out there?"

Nothing.

"Ten? Twenty?"

The man closed his eyes and seemed to drift off to sleep. He was still alive, judging by the slight rise and fall of his chest under his assault vest, though probably not for long. Keo had seen guys who had been gut shot before. It was never pretty, and it never ended well.

"Fine, be an asshole."

Keo unclipped the man's radio, stood up, and jogged off.

He could already hear the other ATVs coming in his direction, having broken off from their previous paths to respond to his gunfire. Good, because he had been afraid they would keep going after Zachary and Shorty.

He picked up his pace, tossing the AK-47 and flicking the fire-selector on the MP5SD from semi-automatic to full-auto. At least he had his weapon back, so things were definitely starting to look up.

After a minute of silently walking back toward the shoreline, following in Zachary and Shorty's footsteps, Keo began to slow down. He could still hear the ATVs coming, but they were still far off.

What am I doing?

Good question. He needed to keep going. Zachary wasn't going to wait forever at the beach with Norris. There was no reason to still be inside the woods after today. He had rescued Norris, and now he could retreat to the island and wait them out. Sooner or later, Pollard (if he was even still alive) would have to leave when their supplies ran low, or when the creatures finally, eventually, broke through the park visitors' building.

So what was he doing, standing still? It was a no-brainer.

Wasn't it?

He didn't know when he decided (or if he did at all; everything was a blur), but soon the radio was in his hand and he had pressed the transmit lever and was lifting it to his lips.

"Pollard," he said into the radio. "You still alive?"

He waited for a response.

He's dead.

Five seconds…

Thank God, he's dead.

Then ten…

See you in hell, Polla—

"You did that," the familiar voice said through the radio. There was no enthusiasm or hate, or even emotion. It was just a simple statement of fact. "Last night. That was you, wasn't it?"

Pollard.

The man was like a cockroach. Then again, he was sure Pollard could say the same thing about him.

"I did," Keo said.

"How?"

"You weren't the only one who wanted a piece of me last night, as it turned out."

"Lou," Pollard said without hesitation.

"I guess I killed his brother or something."

He craned his head and listened for the ATVs. They were either still far off or they had gone in the wrong direction, because he could barely hear them anymore. Keo found himself looking back north, toward where he assumed Pollard was at the moment.

"A lot of that going around these days," Pollard said, "you killing people's loved ones."

Keo smirked. "Fuck you, Pollard. You pull a knife or a gun on me and I'll piss on your bloodline."

"Charming."

"I've been called worse." Then, "Hey, Pollard."

"What?" There was a noticeable agitation in Pollard's voice that time, something that wasn't present before.

The calm is breaking. Let's see how much control you really have, Pollard.

"I'm coming for you," Keo said. "You think I'm going to keep running? Think again. I'm coming, and there's not a goddamn thing you can do about it." He paused and waited for a response. When he didn't get anything after five seconds, Keo continued. "Are you ready for me, old man? This is what you've wanted all along. Who says dreams don't come true, huh?"

"Come on, then," Pollard said. "Let's finish this like the professionals we both are."

"You still think you know me, huh?"

"I know plenty of guys like you."

"You just think you do. That's the funny part."

"We'll see."

"You're right. I'll see you soon, Pollard."

He turned off the radio and hooked it to his hip. Then he turned completely around and began walking north.

Back toward Pollard...

CHAPTER 15

HE DIDN'T BLAME Pollard for wanting him dead. Or for picking up his personal army and chasing him through the Louisiana woods for as long as it took. In the man's shoes, Keo would have done the same thing. From a distance, Pollard looked as if he was in his late forties, maybe early fifties, and while it wasn't too late for him to have another kid, it was definitely too late for him to shape a new son in his image.

And what father didn't want to mold their kid? Keo's dad had wanted the same thing, until it became obvious his son just wasn't interested in following his path. The Army had no allure for Keo, and neither did the old man's strict, disciplinary ways.

So yeah, Keo didn't have any grudges against Pollard, even if the other man probably felt the exact opposite. It was bad enough realizing your bloodline might not survive the end of the world, but to actually have it survive and *then* be snuffed out? That had to be a real kick in the balls.

Of course, understanding Pollard's loss didn't mean Keo wasn't going to put a bullet in the man's head the first chance he got anyway.

Life sucks, then you eat a bullet.

He moved through the woods with purpose, occasionally firing a shot with the Sig Sauer into the air to direct traffic toward him and further away from Zachary, Shorty, and Norris. The trio would already be moving slowly; they didn't need an all-terrain vehicle bearing down on them, too. He, on the other hand, could deal with it.

There were two more ATVs gunning for him that he could hear but not see. Three in all when the morning began. *Just three, though.* That was something of a surprise. He was almost certain Pollard would have more than just three men available after last night. Maybe the bloodsuckers had really done a lot of damage after all?

Sucks to be them.

KEO HAD BEEN walking and shooting into the air for the last five minutes when the second ATV finally found him. The problem with an all-terrain vehicle was that it was loud, and you could hear and feel the damn thing through the ground and even the trees, the branches vibrating as it approached.

It was a red Honda, and there were two riding piggyback this time. The one in the back had his AK-47 raised with the barrel pointing up at the sky. That was useless, because Keo wasn't above them. They were both men—thirties, maybe—and they wore the same black clothes and black assault vest. He wondered if those were all the clothes they had. Probably. It would certainly make dressing in the mornings easier. And there was that whole uniform look. It was something an ex-military guy like Pollard would come up with.

Keo let them ride past him, the drag from the vehicle embracing him in cool air for the first time all morning. He basked in it just long enough to aim and shoot the second man in the back with the newly reacquired MP5SD. The man must have banged his head into the driver after being shot, because the other man jerked on the handlebars and the ATV turned sharply and nearly flipped over. Somehow, the man managed to regain control just in time, and the bike slid to a stop, dirt kicking into the air as the wheels locked up.

As soon as the vehicle came to a stop, Keo shot the driver in the chest, then shot him a second time as he slumped forward before collapsing off the Honda. The man in the back did the same thing, both bodies sliding silently down to the ground.

The ATV was leaking gas, but the engine kept churning for a few seconds before simply shutting off by itself. He guessed he must have hit something vital on it.

Keo remained where he was, standing perfectly still and listening for sounds of the third—and final—pursuit vehicle, but he couldn't detect it over the soft chirping of birds above and the scurrying of creatures along branches around him.

There was nothing out there that didn't belong. A big, fat nothing.

Where did the last ATV go? Did Pollard recall it? That would have been the smart move, and Pollard was smart. He might be gathering his remaining forces back at the park visitors' building right now, knowing Keo was getting closer.

Keo continued north, walking at an unhurried pace.

✳

"*SEE THE WORLD. Kill some people. Make some money.*"

Things had been so simpler then, before the world decided to make his life complicated. He didn't have anyone to worry about except himself, which had worked out for the last ten years.

Then Gillian came along. Then Norris. Then the others.

All of that, because he decided to stop in one lousy Louisiana town one day when he should have kept right on driving. A part of him wondered if he would be running around *with* Pollard now and not against him if he hadn't stopped at Bentley that fateful day.

Maybe. Maybe not. Who the hell knows.

The sound of tiny feet scurrying along a branch above him made him look up. He saw the squirrel—it looked familiar, but of course it couldn't possibly be the same one from that night he spent in the tree, could it?—running along a tree branch.

It was fleeing something—

The man jumped down from the branch where he had been perching for God knew how long, the distance between them about ten meters. His face was covered in a painted white skull, the sight of it like some kind of demon falling out of the sky to claim him. Gleaming black eyes glinted and a smile, like a Cheshire cat's, spread wide.

I know that face!

Keo saw the man a split-second before he made his move. He wouldn't have seen him at all if not for the squirrel. That brief moment was just enough time for Keo to twist partially around, but not quite enough opportunity to lift either the MP5SD or dive out of the man's path.

Knees slammed into his chest with the force of a boulder.

Keo's legs crumpled under him, but he somehow (and he had no idea how) still managed to hook his arm around the man's neck even as their bodies collided in a crush of flesh and limbs and pain. For an instant, the man's skull came within an inch of Keo's.

Up close, Keo was sure he recognized the face.

Jacks.

The one who had hit him in the back of the head with his AK-47. The familiar eyes, that permanently amused grin. Just remembering Jacks made the back of Keo's head tingle. Christ, he hoped he wasn't bleeding back there again, since he had almost forgotten all about it.

Keo willed his entire body to keep twisting, even as the breath exploded out of his lungs, the result of Jacks's knees to his chest. (What the hell did the guy think he was doing, some kind of martial arts movie? Muay Thai, maybe?) He was twisting, twisting—until he got Jacks underneath him as they fell, hard, to the ground.

Keo ended up on top, and even as he struggled to breathe, was the first one to rise.

The sun glinted off the sharp point of a knife in Jacks's hand. Keo picked it up with the corner of one eye. When the hell had he gotten that out? The blade was moving in a wide arc, from right to left, bottom to top, aiming for Keo's head.

Keo struck out with his left hand, batting away the attacking knife. Before Jacks could counter, Keo smashed the heel of his right hand down and into the man's face and felt rather than saw the nose giving way and the warm sensation of liquid *(blood)* splattering across his palm.

Jacks might have grunted. Keo couldn't hear anything anyway. He was too busy ignoring (or trying to ignore) the searing pain blasting across his chest at the moment. Was it possible to break someone's chest cavity? Because that was what it felt like after taking Jacks's knees full-on.

He could barely breathe, but he managed to push aside that fact just long enough to reach down for the Sig Sauer in his hip holster and pull it out. Jacks's eyes widened, even more than before, and that unseemly smile plastered on his face faded for the first time.

"Not fair," Jacks said through gritted teeth. "I could have shot you, but I didn't."

"Your mistake," Keo said—

Knife!

He jerked backward as Jacks slashed with the knife—right at the spot where he had been a millisecond ago. Keo stumbled completely off Jacks's body, lost his footing, and fell on his ass to the ground, even as Jacks attempted to push himself up.

Keo pulled the trigger. It was difficult to miss from less than a meter away. The .45 caliber round entered the bloody spot where Jacks's nose used to be and exited the top of his head. Brain, bone, and blood sprayed the humid air.

Jacks slumped back down to the ground and lay perfectly still. The knife, somehow, was still clutched tightly in his right hand.

Keo struggled back up on wobbly feet, exhausted from the fight, which had lasted—how long? A few seconds? Ten seconds at the most, even if it did feel longer. Like an hour. Or two.

But no, it had only lasted a few seconds. Not even close to a minute.

He holstered the Sig Sauer and staggered forward, seemingly incapable of standing still no matter how hard he tried. Maybe it was the effect of being hit in the back of the head yesterday by Jacks's buttstock coming back with a vengeance. Was he bleeding again back there? He didn't feel blood trickling down, but how much could he really trust his sense of touch at the moment?

Keo had somehow made it to a nearby tree. He leaned against it for support, then slid down to the ground and rested. He wasn't even aware he had the submachine gun positioned in front of him until he looked down and saw it gripped tightly in his hands.

The radio clipped to his hip squawked, the loud mechanical noise making him jump for a moment, before he realized what it was.

A familiar voice said through the radio, "You still alive out there, Keo?"

Keo didn't answer right away. He didn't trust himself to respond. He sucked in more large breaths instead.

"Keo?" Pollard said. "Don't tell me you're dead."

He finally unclipped the radio and held it up to his lips. "Sorry to disappoint you."

How did he sound? Calm? In control? Or was he wheezing just a little bit? It was hard to tell because his ears were ringing for some reason. The good news was that his chest had stopped trying to burn a hole through his body.

"On the contrary," Pollard said, "I'm happy you're still alive."

If Keo had sounded out of breath when he answered, Pollard hadn't picked up on it.

"I'm almost there," Keo said into the radio.

He drew the Sig Sauer and fired a shot into the air. He didn't know why he did it. Why give away his position? It was such a stupid thing to do, and yet, the old Keo came back with a vengeance and he just couldn't stop himself. Hell, he didn't *want* to stop it.

He was going to die anyway, right?

Might as well have a little fun first.

As the gunshot echoed, he said into the radio, "You hear that?"

"You're close," Pollard said.

"I'll be seeing you very soon."

"Don't keep me waiting."

Keo clipped the radio back to his hip and pushed up to his feet, then away from the tree and stumbled forward. It was good to be moving again. For some reason, it felt worse when he was resting, which was a bit of a mystery. Shouldn't it have been the other way around?

Christ, he hoped the stitches on the back of his head hadn't snapped. Maybe Jacks's flying knee strike had been more effective than he wanted to believe—and it had been pretty damn effective already.

He stopped for a moment to catch his breath for the—how many times was that?

He should really feel the back of his head to see if he was bleeding back there.

No. Ignorance is bliss.

Yeah, let's go with that.

✳

THE PARK VISITORS' building was still. Too still. There should have been someone standing around the vehicles still scattered across the yard. From his position, he could make out three ATVs sprinkled among the trucks. There were no sentries on the rooftops this time, and for the next twenty minutes as he sat quietly and watched, he didn't see a single sign of life coming from inside or outside the building.

He hadn't counted the cars when he was here yesterday, so he had no idea if Pollard had taken off in one of them or not. That was unlikely, though. He would have heard the sound of engines as he approached his target if Pollard was retreating.

Not that he expected Pollard to run. The man had chased him for almost three months, committing his fighting force in the name of revenge. Whether Pollard was in that building by himself or surrounded by his men at this very moment, he wasn't going anywhere anytime soon. Not while Keo was still alive, anyway.

Who's the dummy here? Him or me?

Maybe both.

Nah, definitely me.

He positioned the submachine gun in front of him, and making sure he was still invisible inside the tree line, unclipped the radio and pressed the transmit lever. "Come out, come out, wherever you are."

He lowered the radio and waited for a response.

Five seconds passed.

Then ten…

"I'm disappointed in you, Pollard," Keo said into the radio. "I expected you to be waiting for me outside the yard for one of those old-fashioned Mexican standoffs. But I don't see you anywhere. You're not hiding from little ol' me, are you?"

Another five seconds.

Then another ten…

"All right, then," Keo said. "Let's do this the hard way."

He stood up—

Crunch-crunch-crunch!

He spun around, just in time to see a dark black shape smash into his chest, almost at the exact same spot where he had been kneed less than half an hour ago by Jacks.

What is this, kick Keo in the chest day?

The radio went flying out of his hand and his mind was still spinning when he felt the brutally cold steel—all five inches of it—sinking into his side. The blade only stopped its penetration after it ran out of steel and there was just the plastic handle of the knife bumping up against his skin.

Pollard, his face a mask of something that could be anger, pain, misery, or possibly just raw determination, picked Keo up from the ground and threw him out into the open yard with a loud, inhuman howl.

"Die!" Pollard shouted, stalking out of the tree line after him. "Why won't you fucking die already?"

CHAPTER 16

GODDAMN, THAT'S RED, was the thought that ran through Keo's mind when he saw his blood coating the tactical knife gripped in Pollard's right fist. For some reason, it never occurred to him that his blood would be that bright and that red. Then again, it could just be the crisp glare of the morning sun playing havoc with his vision.

Or the pain. Yeah, it was probably the pain.

Pollard's fingers were clenched so tightly around the brown handle of the eleven-inch weapon that they had turned pale white. The man's face remained contorted in that odd expression—a mixture of hate and exhilaration—as he walked toward Keo, as if he had all the time in the world, and not at all like a father about to exact his long sought-after revenge against the man responsible.

Keo had lost the MP5SD. Between being picked up and tossed out of the woods (as if he were a child, which was pretty damn embarrassing) into the front yard of the park visitors' building and flying through the air, the submachine gun had been dislodged despite the strap. He could see the steel suppressor jutting up from the blades of overgrown grass between him and Pollard. No way he could reach it in time before Pollard gutted him.

The Sig Sauer was also gone, and Keo couldn't figure out how that had happened. Unlike the Heckler & Koch, though, the .45 was lost somewhere among the weeds. It was going to take a miracle to find it again.

His fingers were covered in *(his)* blood when he groped for and found the handle of the Ka-Bar knife. Lou's. Or Chris's. Either/or.

He slid it out of its sheath as he picked himself up from the ground. He expected Pollard to bull-rush him again, but the man actually slowed down, content to let Keo get up. It could be that the ex-officer was being sporting. Or maybe he was just confident.

Keo looked down at his left side. His shirt was soaked and blood trickled out through the small cut (almost invisible to the naked eye) in the fabric. The knife had gone in deep. All five inches of it. At least it hadn't punctured anything vital, so the only thing he had to worry about was bleeding to death.

And the pain, of course.

Goddamn, there was a lot of pain.

"I didn't know you did the dirty work yourself, Pollard," Keo said.

How did he sound? Out of breath? Rushed? Hurt? He couldn't tell by Pollard's expression. The man had stopped moving and was standing a meter away from him. So close that Keo could hear the vengeful father's haggard breathing. Or was that his *own* breathing?

Either/or.

"Now who's being presumptuous?" Pollard said. "You

don't know me from Adam, son."

Up close, Pollard looked older than he had expected. He might have been in his fifties, but the pained expression on his face made his lines more noticeable and tightened his eyes too severely. He had flecks of gray sprinkled among his short hair and a growing stubble. There was something else—a fresh red scar across his right cheek that looked like a perfect line. A bullet graze.

I guess I didn't miss completely, after all.

"I think I know you enough," Keo said.

"You have no idea," Pollard said.

He was an inch shorter than Keo, but he was muscular, the kind of strength that came with years of hard work. Keo wasn't looking at a commissioned officer who had spent his time in the office while his men sweated in the sun. Pollard knew physical labor, and it showed in the way he had effortlessly lifted Keo up and tossed him around.

Goddamn, he's strong.

"Where I've been," Pollard continued. "What I've seen." His mouth twisted into a smile. "But you will!"

He charged, the knife slashing.

It was a good strike, the kind that came with a lot of practice. Unlike with Lou last night, there was no Primal Mode here. This was a calculated attack with a lot of thought behind it. It didn't surprise Keo at all that Pollard was ex-military. He would have guessed as much even if he hadn't known the man's past from Fiona.

Keo's Ka-Bar was two inches longer than Pollard's knife, but that extra length was useless. It didn't help that he was slow to react, moving almost as if he were stuck in molasses. It was the pain and the bleeding, both of it coming from his left side where Pollard's knife had already taken a big chunk out of him.

Yeah, that's it. That's the reason.

He barely managed to parry the slashing blade, but even as he sidestepped it, Pollard quickly readjusted his forward momentum and elbowed Keo in the face. He staggered back, more stunned than hurt, expecting to feel blood rushing down his nose at any second.

It was broken, wasn't it?

Maybe not, because there was no river of blood pouring into his mouth. Not that the lack of the red stuff made the pain any less, because there was a lot of that, as if something had exploded inside his head. He did the best he could to fight his way through it, but it wasn't nearly enough. Not even close.

Keo was busy stumbling backward, still reeling from the blow. Somewhere along the way, he had lost the Ka-Bar.

Shit. Where did it go?

Pollard was righting himself before darting in for another attempt. This time he came within half an inch of slicing open Keo's forehead. Keo managed to snap his head back just in time as the blade (still covered in his blood, no less) flashed across his face.

The Ka-Bar. Where the hell is that knife?

Here, little Ka-Bar. Here, little Ka-Bar...

He struck out with his left hand, his only available option given their positions, and hit Pollard across the face. If he thought that was going to do anything, he was sadly mistaken. Pollard shook it off as if it were nothing and followed Keo, smashing his meaty left fist into Keo's face.

That threw Keo for another loop, and he stupidly lowered

his guard.

Pollard took advantage of the opening. He lunged and barreled his shoulder into Keo for the second time. Keo had no ability to resist and he went down, hard. The back of his head slammed into the ground and the universe seemed to cave in on him.

Oh yeah, that's gonna snap those stitches, all right.

Then Pollard was on top of him, straddling his waist. The older man punched Keo in the face again, using the same fist that was clutching the knife.

Keo grunted, felt blood this time, and knew his nose was broken.

Pollard grabbed a handful of Keo's hair and cocked back his knife to finish it. His face was wild, eyes bulging, the composure starting to disappear. Keo could see the Primal Mode starting to assert itself. And there was just the ghost of a smile on his lips, which somehow made it even worse.

"This is it, Keo!" Pollard shouted. "This is three months in the making! You ready, son? You ready to get what you have coming to you?"

Oh, shut up, Keo thought, and managed to reach up with his right hand and slip his fingers around Pollard's throat, while his left snaked out and snatched the wrist holding the knife that was arcing toward his head.

Keo was hurt. His world was collapsing in on him. The burning fire in his left side hadn't gone down since Pollard drove the knife into it. That, combined with the roaring pain from his broken nose, made him want to give in right then and there. But he didn't. Because he couldn't.

Gillian would so kick my ass.

He could taste his own blood dripping into his mouth. He just hoped the nose wasn't too badly broken. Maybe he could reset it later. Didn't girls dig guys with broken noses? Maybe Gillian was one of those gals—

"Die!" Pollard shouted, somehow managing to get the word out despite Keo's fingers tightening around his throat. "Die already! Why won't you just die?"

Pollard must have summoned every ounce of strength he possessed. Maybe he even dug deep down and found more, because Keo was losing the fight. Pollard's right hand was moving, the knife traveling an inch closer and closer toward Keo's—

He screamed when the point of the blade dug into his left cheek and drew blood. He didn't cry out so much from the pain but from the surprise of having a steel instrument penetrating his skin and seeing it happen with the corner of his eye.

"For Joe!" Pollard shouted. "This is for my son!"

Keo was choking the life out of the man. So how the hell was Pollard seemingly getting stronger and stronger with every second, while he got weaker and weaker? How was any of this possible?

The only thing keeping Pollard from driving all five inches of the knife into Keo's cheek was Keo's hand, holding it back. *Barely.*

That is, until Pollard decided if he couldn't go in, he would go up, and began pushing the double-bladed knife *up* instead of *in.*

The alien feel of the cold instrument slicing into his flesh sent all kinds of sensations coursing through Keo's body. He wanted to scream out again, but couldn't figure out how to do it this time. Maybe it was the pain from his side, or the one from the back of his head, or the knife cutting open his face at this very moment—

"Die!" Pollard shouted. "Just fucking die already!"

"No!" Keo shouted back. "Fuck you, and fuck Joe!"

He didn't know how he had managed that little comeback. It must have also taken Pollard by surprise, because his eyes widened even further (was that even possible?) and the brutal mask of hate and anger and fury seemed to slip.

It wasn't for very long—maybe a *half second*—but it was long enough that Pollard briefly stopped carving Keo's face like a jack-o'-lantern.

Now now now!

Keo let go of Pollard's neck, pulled his arm back, and punched the man in the throat. Pollard gagged and the knife cutting into the side of Keo's face disappeared momentarily. It was just enough time for Keo to lift his entire body slightly off the ground, twist left, and cock his right arm in the air before driving it back and smashing the elbow into the side of Pollard's neck.

He swore he heard something break as Pollard's entire body seemed to go slack and he toppled sideways off Keo, landing in the grass on his side. Keo rolled away, then fumbled up to his knees and looked over at Pollard, expecting the man to get right back up, too, with the knife in his fist ready to finish the job.

But Pollard was lying on the ground, his head turned at an awkward angle. His hand, still gripping the knife, twitched, as if he kept trying to move it, to strike out at Keo, but couldn't make it obey. His eyes remained intensely focused on Keo, though, and his lips quivered but no words or sounds came out.

Keo stumbled up to his feet. Blood was flowing in rivulets out of the cut along the left side of his face. He didn't know how deep or long the cut was, but there was enough blood to know it was just deep and long enough. He put his hand over his left side, where Pollard had knifed him earlier. His palm was instantly slick, telling him he was going to need something better to stanch the bleeding than just blood-soaked fingers.

Pollard wasn't dead, but he looked halfway there. He might have been paralyzed. Or, at least, he didn't appear to be breathing anymore.

Keo crouched next to the man and stared back at him. "You should have left me alone."

Pollard's lips quivered, but no words came out.

"I'm sorry about your son," Keo continued. "But Joe was a piece of shit and he deserved everything he got."

Pollard's body trembled and his eyes snapped shut.

Keo had seen men die in worse ways than what Pollard was going through. Some of those moments were the result of his handiwork. He thought he was used to it, up close and personal, but this…

He stood up. He didn't need or want to see this play out.

He staggered around, looking for his weapons instead. He found the MP5SD nearby and slung it with some effort, trying not to pass out when he leaned down for the submachine gun, then again when he straightened back up. He couldn't find the Sig Sauer anywhere, but did locate the Ka-Bar after about ten seconds of looking around. If it had been any better hidden, he would never have found it. Thank God it was nearby.

He looked over when he thought Pollard might have said something. But the man was looking in the wrong direction, and whatever sound had come out of his mouth had gotten lost in the late summer heat. *If* he had said anything at all. It might have all been in Keo's head.

"Hey," a voice said.

That one was definitely *not* in his head.

Keo turned around, fumbling with the MP5SD. Or he thought he was. He was in so much pain, and everything had gone so numb that he could have been flexing against the air and wouldn't have known the difference.

"You look like shit," a short figure standing next to him said.

It was a woman. Or a girl. Definitely female.

The sun was in his eyes, so he couldn't really make her out. She looked small and frail, or maybe the brightness of the open field was playing tricks with his mind. God knew the pain was overwhelming every single one of his senses at the moment.

"Yeah?" he managed to say.

"Yeah," the figure said. "You gonna die now?"

"I think so," Keo said, and fell into the grass.

He might have slammed into the ground on his face, or his cheek, or actually managed to summon forth some still-remaining sense of self-preservation and reached out with his arms to stop his fall just in time. He couldn't really be sure, and at that moment, he didn't really give a damn.

The ground felt warm against his face, though that could have just been the blood.

Either/or.

CHAPTER 17

THOOM-THOOM-THOOM.

He was swimming in a fog filled with mud and pain. Throbbing, piercing pain. The kind that made you want to never open your eyes again.

Thoom-thoom-thoom.

He had no idea how long he had been asleep. The fact that he was waking up at all was a miracle. He was supposed to be dead. Right now, he wouldn't mind a permanent—and most importantly, peaceful—rest.

Thoom-thoom-thoom.

There was that damn awful sound again. What was it? Flesh hitting wood?

Thoom-thoom-thoom.

He wished it would stop. It was bad enough he couldn't breathe without feeling like his ribcage was going to implode. Keo had been shot, stabbed, and at one point almost paralyzed before, but no one had ever tried to cut off his face with a five-inch blade. That was a new one.

Thoom-thoom-thoom.

"Goddammit," he said out loud.

"Relax," a female voice said. The woman from earlier, who had appeared out of nowhere after his little dust-up with—

Pollard.

Dead now. Keo had broken his neck. Snapped a vertebrae or two (or three) and cut off his breathing. It was a hell of a way to go, and Keo didn't feel the least bit sorry for the guy. Well, maybe just a little bit.

No one told you to chase me through half of Louisiana, asshole.

He opened his eyes to semidarkness. Thin slivers of moonlight pierced pieces of furniture that had been upended against a window at the back of the room. A metal filing cabinet, chairs stacked on top of one another, and a sofa. There was no real order, as if whoever had put the barricade together simply shoved as much as they could find against the opening and hoped for the best.

Thoom-thoom-thoom!

The figure leaning over him looked concerned. Stringy blonde hair fell across an oval-shaped face and brown eyes that still managed to look bright in the dark room. "You really lost a lot of blood. I didn't think you'd make it."

Keo couldn't move. He didn't want to move, either. Every rise and fall of his chest sent a stabbing pain from the tip of his toes all the way up to his damp head. He felt the chill of medical ointment over the left side of his face, which was now covered in a strip of bandage. A long strip of bandage. He didn't want to touch it, because that would tell him just how long it really was.

Maybe Gillian will like it. Scars add character, right?

"Where am I?" he asked. His voice sounded muffled, like he was talking through a mouthful of cotton.

Thanks for the broken nose, Pollard.

He could feel the break at the bridge of his nose, but it didn't really hurt. He wasn't entirely sure if that was a good thing or a bad thing.

"Inside one of the offices in the first building," the woman *(girl)* said. "We dragged you in here. Brian wanted to shoot you, but I talked him out of it."

"We should have shot him," a male voice said from somewhere in the background. "That was Pollard's order."

"Pollard's dead," the girl said sharply. Despite her age, she was clearly in charge. "Nothing he says matters anymore. He's the one who dragged us down here from Corden in the first place. Rupert's dead because of him, too."

Rupert.

The kid who had been patrolling with Fiona when he stumbled across them yesterday. (Or was that two days ago? He was losing track of the days again...) The last time he saw the teenager, he was keeling over after getting shot in the gut by his own people.

Which would make the girl Georgette.

"We found him and his sister hiding in a cellar near Corden," Fiona had said. *"They'd been there since all of this began."*

The teenager gave him a half-smile. It wasn't completely friendly, but it was far from malevolent. "Stitching you up is becoming a habit, mister. What kind of name is Keo, anyway?"

"Gary was taken," he said. Then, "You've done this before?"

"What's that? Stitch you up?"

"Yes."

"I'm the one who sewed your head back together last night. That means I've saved your life twice now."

"Thank you."

"You're welcome."

Thoom-thoom-thoom.

He had forgotten about the creatures outside the office, but they hadn't forgotten about them. Keo looked over as much of the room as he could from his supine angle on the floor. It was one of the offices near the front of the building. He recognized it because he and Norris had gone through all of them the first day they arrived at the park. The door was locked down with a large oak desk and a pile of furniture behind it. From the clothes and boxes of supplies lying around, he guessed that at one point there had been more people in here. Until last night, anyway.

Thoom-thoom-thoom.

The legs of the desk were pointing back at him, the flat top pressed against the doorframe. The heavy furniture quivered each time the creatures smashed into the door from the other side, but it held, thanks to chairs and an old white sofa shoved against it as additional reinforcement.

Thoom-thoom-thoom.

He and Georgette weren't alone in the room. Besides Brian, the man *(boy)* whose voice Keo had heard earlier, there were two other women. The oldest looked to be in her twenties with short hair. She sat huddled in one corner, arms thrown over her knees, staring at the floor. If it were possible, she would have merged with the wall at her back. Her entire body fidgeted in tune to the *thoom-thoom-thoom!*

The fourth person in the room was Brian and Georgette's age. They were all teenagers, though they looked older these days. They had grown up fast, but their youth still peeked through the dirt and anxiety, even in the darkened room.

Brian sat next to the window, clutching an AR-15. Blue eyes pierced the darkness back at Keo. The attempt at intimidation was there, but the kid didn't have it in him to make it work. He was the only one in the room wearing a gun belt and black clothes. Georgette, along with the other two girls, was in cargo pants and a T-shirt. All four *(five)* of them were slicked with sweat inside the sealed room.

Thoom-thoom-thoom.

He was lying on some kind of blanket. He wasn't surprised to see his gun belt, MP5SD, and Ka-Bar knife (still in its sheath) resting in a pile next to Brian. They had also taken his watch for some reason.

"What time is it?" Keo asked.

"Does it matter?" Georgette said. "It's night."

Keo didn't press the question. She was right. It didn't matter. Night was night, and when darkness came, *they* came…

A sudden rush of pain made him clench his teeth.

"Here," Georgette said as she took out something from her pocket. She reached down and pulled his head up from the floor.

"What is it?" he asked.

"Something for the pain."

He opened his mouth and let her deposit the octagon-shaped pill onto his tongue. He eagerly swallowed it.

Pain, pain, go away…

She laid him back down. "You really lost a lot of blood."

"You mentioned that…"

"What I mean is, you're probably not going to live through the night."

He somehow managed to smile up at her.

She looked back at him, confused. "Why are you smiling? I just told you you're probably going to die before morning."

Gillian, he thought, but was unable to turn her name into actual sounds. Instead, he closed his eyes and went to sleep. Either the pill was having an effect, or the pain was becoming unbearable.

Either/or.

He didn't particularly care which one it was. Sleep was sleep. And right now he needed as much of it as he could get, even with the bloodsuckers knocking on the window and door, trying to get in at them.

Keep at it, boys. Keep right on at it.

I'm gonna go to sleep for a bit while you keep on keeping on...

"I DIDN'T KILL your brother," Keo said a few hours later.

He wasn't sure how long he had slept, but it felt like another lifetime ago that he had first woken up inside the office surrounded by monsters outside the door. His entire body seemed recharged. Then again, it could have just been the pill she had given him.

Either/or.

It was impossibly silent not just inside the room, but outside the building as well. The creatures, Georgette said when he woke up, had stopped trying to get in about thirty minutes earlier, though she still refused to tell him the time for some reason. Maybe she thought he was going to die before morning and didn't want to give him false hope. Or maybe she was just being slightly vindictive and didn't want to give him something he had asked for twice now.

It remained dark inside the room, except for the thin slivers of moonlight that managed to make their way through the haphazardly put together window barricade. Keo could just barely make out Brian, dozing off next to the window, the AR-15 lying dangerously across his lap with the barrel pointed at Keo. He wondered if that was on purpose or just a not-so-happy coincidence.

"I know," Georgette said, after a while. She was sitting somewhere next to him against the wall. "Darren told me."

"Who's Darren?"

"He's the guy who shot Rupert. He said it was an accident, that he thought my brother was you."

"He told you that himself?"

"Yes. He was crying when he did."

"What happened to Darren?"

"He died last night when those creatures got inside." She paused, then, "A lot of people died last night."

Keo didn't say anything.

"I guess you got lucky those things found a way in," Georgette said.

"Yeah," he said. "I guess I did."

He wondered if she was looking at him this very moment, trying to gauge his reaction. He hoped not. Keo had never been a particularly good liar, and he wasn't sure he could hide his culpability in last night's massacre if she was eyeballing him at close range.

"Pollard would have really made you suffer, you know," the teenager said. "That's why he insisted you stay alive that night.

He wanted to kill you himself, for killing Joe."

"I had no choice with Joe."

"Yeah, I figured. He was kind of an asshole, anyway. Charming one second, and smarmy the next. I never really liked him that much. I don't think anybody did."

May you rot in hell, Joe, you lying little shit.

"Why did you save me?" Keo asked. "After everything that's happened?"

"We didn't want to be here, chasing after you and the black guy. But we didn't have a choice. Rupert said we hitched our wagon to Pollard, so now we have to ride along wherever they go, even if it means leaving the others behind in Corden. So here we are. Now that Pollard's dead, though…" She shrugged. "It was his vendetta, not ours. I don't care if you live or die, honestly."

"You saved my life, so you must care a little."

She sighed. "It's not in my nature to let someone die if I can save them. Thank your lucky stars."

"I'll just thank you instead."

"Whatever."

"How many more survivors are still left in Corden?"

"About fifty stayed behind. Pollard only brought the ones he considers his soldiers. Me, Darlene, and Justine are part of their support staff. My dad was a vet, and I used to work with him all the time at his clinic. He taught me a lot, and I guess I'm the closest thing Pollard has to a doctor. Sad, I know. Darlene and Justine cooked and cleaned for them. Which is why we're going back to Corden tomorrow."

"Why didn't you leave earlier today, after Pollard died?"

"Duh," she said, sounding so young that it momentarily

took him by surprise. "I wanted to make sure you didn't die first, you idiot."

Keo smiled. "Thank you. Again."

She frowned. "I still don't think you're going to make it to morning."

"I've been known to buck the odds."

"Yeah, I can see that."

Talking was easier for him than moving, but not by much. He continued to ache all over, though the pain from his side seemed to have lessened noticeably. Unfortunately, the entire left side of his face probably wasn't going to stop tingling anytime soon.

"Die! Why won't you fucking die already?" Pollard had shouted at him.

Screw you, old man. I got a promise to keep.

THE LOUD *CRACK!* of a rifle snapped Keo awake, the fog that had been floating around inside his skull throughout the day lifting instantly. Or at least, that's what he told himself as he sprang up from the floor and cursed the resulting ripple of pain.

Brian and Georgette were at the window, peering through the small spaces left open around the barricade. It was still dark—probably early morning. Past midnight, he was sure of it.

"Did you get them?" Georgette asked.

"I don't know," Brian said. He pulled his AR-15 from a hole and shook his head. "Maybe. I don't know."

"How many did you see?"

"Two? Maybe three?"

"Well, which one is it? Two or three?"

"Jesus, I don't know, Georgie. Either two or three, okay?"

Georgette sighed. "I think they went back into the woods. I don't see them anymore."

"I might have gotten one of them," Brian said. He sounded as if he were trying to convince himself. "That must be why they're retreating."

"What's happening?" Keo asked.

Georgette glanced back at him. "There were men outside, wearing some kind of white—" she turned back to Brian "—what did you call it?"

"Hazmat suits," Brian said. "I've seen it in the movies. But not that bulky kind. These were sleek, like soldiers would wear. They were carrying rifles and I'm pretty sure I saw one of them with a gun belt."

"And masks, right?"

"Right. They were wearing gas masks, too."

Keo looked at Georgette, then over at Brian. Or the back of Brian's head, because the teenager hadn't looked away from the peephole, his AR15 still clutched tightly in his hands.

"You don't believe me?" Georgette said.

No, Keo thought, but said, "Men in hazmat suits and gas masks? Out there at night?"

"It's true." She sounded slightly annoyed. "You can believe me or not, but we've seen them before, back at Corden."

"What did they want?"

"How the hell should I know?" She turned back to the window and said to Brian, "You see them?"

"No," Brian said, shaking his head. "I think I scared them off—"

Pop-pop-pop!

The wooden sections of the barricade splintered as bullets punched through them, the loud burst of automatic gunfire filling the night, so chaotic and sudden that it made everyone in the room, including Keo, jump slightly.

Brian lunged to the floor while Georgette spun away from the window and threw her hands over her head. Keo stayed down as a couple of stray rounds made it through the furniture, flew past him, and speckled the wall on the other side. Chunks of wood filled the air and more than a few *ping-ping!* off the heavy metal filing cabinet.

Darlene and Justine, the other two girls, were huddled in the dark corner together, arms and legs tangled. Keo would have thought there was just one person in there if he didn't know there were, in fact, two.

Brian crawled along the floor and got behind a wall. "Holy shit!" he shouted over the gunfire.

It continued for a few more minutes, telling Keo that there was definitely more than one shooter outside. There had to be at least two, or even three, as Brian had guessed. Of course, he didn't understand why they were shooting at the window when they clearly knew they weren't going to knock the barricade down from the other side. The furniture, mixed in with the cabinet, was at least a good 200 to 300 pounds—

He looked toward the door, moving so fast that he regretted it immediately. Pain flashed through him again, but he managed to shove them aside and shouted at Brian, "The door! It's a distraction! Watch the door!"

Brian stared back at him, wide-eyed. He looked as if he were still trying to process what Keo was saying when something massive slammed into the other side of the door.

It sounded like a hammer.

Or maybe a sledgehammer.

BOOM!

CHAPTER 18

"THE DOOR, BRIAN!" Georgette shouted. "The door!"

If Keo's warning hadn't done it, Georgette's voice had a different effect. Brian scrambled up from the floor and ran across the room. Georgette was racing alongside him, and the two threw themselves into the smooth underbelly of the large desk to keep it pinned against the door.

BOOM!

The desk shook with every blow, as if every bloodsucker outside the door was smashing into it with everything they had all at the same time. Keo had never seen the creatures muster that kind of force. They weren't strong. Whatever had happened to them, whatever had stripped them of their humanity, hadn't given them any special strength.

So how were they exerting so much force?

Maybe it wasn't them. Maybe it was something else. The blows took a while. It wasn't the rapid-fire *thoom-thoom-thoom* that he was used to. No. This was more deliberate, as if whoever *(whatever)* was wielding the blunt object—and it had to be an object; flesh and bone couldn't make that kind of noise—had to summon a lot of strength for every blow.

A sledgehammer. It had to be a sledgehammer. Or something else equally large and capable of that kind of force—

BOOM!

Then something else occurred to him and Keo looked back at the window. He hadn't realized it until a few seconds ago, but the gunfire had stopped just after the attack on the door began.

He stumbled up to his feet even as another *BOOM!* sent Georgette reeling. She gathered herself and lunged back into position, pushing the desk into the door with her entire body. Brian was doing the same thing. Looking at them, Keo couldn't fend off the image of two kids trying to hold back a dam. It was only a matter of time...

He snatched up his MP5SD from the floor. It was still loaded and he moved toward the window and peered out through one of the dozen or so new holes that had been punched into the wooden sections of the barricade by the last round of gunfire. His eye hadn't fully adjusted to the darkness when—

BOOM!

Something equally heavy and equally destructive slammed into the window and actually made the heavy filing cabinet tremble slightly. A two-pronged attack!

Keo stuck the MP5SD's long suppressor into one of the holes near the middle of the window, where he would expect to find a target, and squeezed the trigger.

He was rewarded by what sounded like a man's scream.

He leaned forward and peered through another one of the openings.

The hell...?

Two figures—both wearing white hazmat suits that clung to their bodies—were moving away from the window. One was on the ground while the other one was pulling him backward by the shoulders. They were both armed, with rifles slung over their belts, gun belts with hip holsters, and gas masks that covered their faces, the breathing apparatus jutting out like tusks. An abandoned sledgehammer, the metal gleaming in the moonlight, lay on the grass.

The sight of the two figures retreating was unreal, and for just a moment Keo wondered if he was still unconscious and this was all just a very strange dream. Or maybe he had never survived his confrontation with Pollard and this was some kind of purgatory reserved especially for guys like him, men with too much blood on their hands.

No. This is real.

Right?

There was a flurry of movement just before a third white figure appeared out of the corner of his right eye. Keo dived to the floor as an AK-47 clattered outside and the wooden barrier splintered. Bullets *zip-zip-zipped* past his head and across the room.

"Shit!" he heard Georgette shout from behind him. He looked back and saw her ducking as the bullets from the window slammed into the wall next to her.

Keo scrambled back up and slid against the wall. There wasn't enough space in the barricade for him to be able to see out, much less shoot back at the men in hazmat suits. But they had stopped firing, probably because they didn't think they could hit him and were too busy dragging their wounded comrade to safety. Of course, maybe they were just waiting for him to poke his head into their line of fire like the idiot he clearly was.

He switched the submachine gun to semi-automatic and stayed where he was, flat against the wall. His ammo pouches were still on the floor next to his gun belt and sheathed Ka-Bar, but Keo didn't reach for them. He also didn't feel any urgent need to leave the wall and get shot by three guys in hazmat suits *(Hazmat suits!)* armed with assault rifles outside.

He looked across the room at Brian instead. The teenager was pressed up against the belly of the desk, staring back at him. For a moment, he wondered if Brian was going to reach for his weapon at the sight of Keo with his. But the kid didn't, which was a good thing because Keo would have easily killed him, and that was the last thing he wanted to do tonight.

"Keo?" Georgette said. She was standing next to Brian, still pushing against the desk with her whole body, even though, like with the window, the attack against the door had stopped.

"I think they're retreating," Keo said.

"Who?"

"Your men in hazmat suits."

She grinned triumphantly. "I told you."

"Yeah, yeah."

He leaned toward the window and looked through the closest hole in the barricade, ears perked up for sounds. Any sound. There was none, and he only saw an empty moonlit yard from the limited angle.

He moved closer and found a bigger peephole with a better view.

Still empty. Still no men in hazmat suits. Or creatures, for that matter. That didn't make any sense at all. Where did they all go?

"There's no one out there," he said, slipping back behind

the wall.

"Who the hell were they?" Georgette asked.

Keo shook his head. "You tell me. You said you've seen them before."

"I didn't actually see them. I heard about them. It sounded crazy at the time, too."

"What did you hear?"

"Druthers said he shot one of them," Brian said. It had been so long since he spoke that the sound of his voice momentarily surprised Keo.

"Who's Druthers?" Keo asked.

"One of Pollard's ex-soldiers," Georgette said. Then, to Brian, "What else did Druthers say?"

"I think it was just a skirmish or something," Brian said. "They were poking their heads around Corden. Druthers didn't know what happened to the guy he shot."

"This was in the daytime?" Keo asked.

Brian nodded. "Yeah. In the afternoon."

"What else?"

"That's it. He didn't really go into details."

"You?" Keo said to Georgette. "What did you hear?"

"Most of it was secondhand," Georgette said. "I was told they were searching the city, looking for something. I guess they saw there were too many of us and decided not to push their luck. That's what I heard, anyway."

"Do you think…" Brian started to say.

"What?" Georgette said.

"Do you think they were working with the bloodsuckers? I mean, how else are they out there at night?"

Georgette didn't answer. Neither did Keo.

"Crazy," Brian said, mostly to himself.

Understatement of the century, kid, Keo thought, but he said instead, "You two stay over there, and I'll watch the window from this moment on."

Georgette and Brian exchanged a look before they both reluctantly nodded.

"Now," Keo said to Georgette, "would you mind telling me what time it is?"

She dug into one of her cargo pants pockets and tossed his watch across the room. Keo snatched it out of the air.

3:14 A.M.

"We should have left this afternoon when we had the chance," Brian said to no one in particular.

Georgette didn't respond. She sat down on the floor next to the door, while Brian did the same on the other side. They both looked tired. And young. He hadn't fully appreciated just how young they both were until now, as they stared off at nothing and wiped at their sweat-slicked faces.

"We'll be okay," Keo said.

They both looked up at him, and he could see that they wanted badly to believe him.

"I've been in worse situations," he continued. "True story: There was this crazy jackass with a small army of heavily-armed men chasing me through the woods for the last three months..."

THE MEN IN the white hazmat suits didn't come back the rest of the night. Keo waited, and so did Brian and Georgette. Even

Darlene and Justine, still huddled somewhere in the dark corner, seemed to be expecting something to happen at any moment to break the monotony of silence, where the only sound was their combined labored and anxious breathing.

Instead, there was just the deadening quiet.

Keo eventually sat down on the floor, while Georgette scooted across the room and checked on his side. Even though the entire left part of his face was still throbbing, he didn't tell her about it. He wasn't going to bleed to death from the cut, even if the initial point of entry was deep enough to really hurt. The knife wound in his side was another story. Pollard had sunk all five inches of cold steel into him down there, and just thinking about it made him grimace.

"Am I hurting you?" Georgette asked as she poked around.

"No," Keo said. "Just bad memories."

"Well, you didn't break my stitches."

"What about the back of my head?"

She checked. "The new bandage I put on last night's still dry, which means the stitches are still good."

"You learned all this while helping your dad at his veterinarian's clinic?"

"You'd be surprised how much harder it is to work on animals than humans. Compared to them, we're domesticated sheep." She sat back on her haunches. "I guess I'm better at this than I thought."

"Your dad would be proud."

"I hope so," she said quietly.

"What about him?" Keo said, nodding across the room at Brian, who stared at the door as if he expected the attack to resume at any second.

THE FIELDS OF LEMURIA 221

"He's sort of my bodyguard," Georgette said. "He goes everywhere I go. I told you. I'm the closest thing Pollard has to a doctor." Then, "How's the nose?"

"Still broken, but it'll heal. They say a broken nose gives you character."

"Yeah, keep telling yourself that."

He chuckled. "You've done a lot of this for Pollard?"

"Rupert and I didn't join a Boy Scout troop. We knew what we were getting into, but it was better than the alternative."

Her face changed noticeably at Rupert's name, and she seemed to drift off.

"I'm sorry about your brother," Keo said. "He seemed like a good kid."

"You were there when it happened?"

"I was."

"Was it an accident, like Darren said?"

Keo thought about it. Standing there, listening to Fiona, with Rupert between them. Then the gunfire. Fiona going down, and a moment later, Rupert doubling over.

"I think so, yeah," Keo said. "They opened up from behind some trees, so they might not have been able to see everyone clearly."

"Fiona, too?"

"Her, too."

"I liked her. She looked after us when we first joined." She sighed and leaned back against the wall.

They didn't say anything for a while. Keo looked across the room at Brian. He had clearly heard everything because he was still wide awake, though he didn't say a word and stared off at something along one of the walls instead.

"You're going back to Corden after this?" Keo asked.

"Yeah," Georgette said. "We were going to take one of the trucks and head back. Brian thinks if we just head north, we should run across Corden eventually."

"Eventually," Keo repeated. He didn't like the sound of that. "But you don't know for sure. Do you have a map?"

"A couple of the guys had maps, but we couldn't find them after last night. They probably had it on them, and when they disappeared…"

Keo nodded. You didn't die anymore. You just turned. You became one of *them.*

So what did that make the people in the hazmat suits and gas masks?

Who the hell were those guys?

"There's another option," Keo said. "You like fish?"

THEY MADE IT through the morning without incident. The men in hazmat suits didn't return, and the creatures stayed away. None of it made any sense, but then, what did these days?

The fact that it was sunlight didn't mean they were safe, though. He had to remind himself that they had been engaged in a gunfight with men last night, and men didn't have to fear the day.

They came out of the building around eight, and Keo stood aside and listened to Brian and Georgette arguing about what to do next. The boy wanted to leave for Corden, but Georgette wanted to go with Keo. At times things got heated, and Brian brought up Rupert's death and those of the others. He (rightfully) accused Keo of being the cause for all their misery and losses.

Smart kid.

Keo let them go at it for a good thirty minutes before Georgette finally said, "If you wanna go, then go." Then she turned to Darlene and Justine. "You guys can go with him, if you want. I'm going with Keo for now."

The other two girls were indecisive, but eventually decided it couldn't hurt to come with Keo, too. He wasn't sure if that was because they thought he was a better protector than Brian or they just liked the idea of an island that was safe from the creatures. Either way, Brian let out some choice curses and kicked the door on one of the trucks. When that was over with, he picked up what supplies they had managed to salvage from the last two nights and followed Keo and the others into the woods. Keo carried as much as he could while the girls dragged along the rest.

It took them four long hours of walking slowly to finally reach the southern shore. Keo didn't want to rush it. There was no need and he was wary of an ambush. God knew he had walked into too many already, even when he knew it was waiting for him. That made him, he reminded himself, one of the dumbest men alive.

Lucky. You got real lucky the last few days, pal.

The image of the men in hazmat suits flashed across his mind's eye every few minutes. It reminded him that there were things going on out there in the rest of the world that he didn't fully understand even now. But then, where had he been since the end of the world? Most of it had been spent in the luxury of Earl's house, with the rest of it running through one Louisiana woods after another, trying to stay ahead of Pollard. It wasn't as if he had time to actually explore the state, much less the country beyond.

Who the hell were those guys?

Finally, they stepped through the trees and onto a stretch of beach. He didn't have binoculars, but he thought he knew where the island was and looked for it among the flickering lake surface.

"Here?" Georgette said behind him.

Keo nodded. "Sit down and rest for a while. I'll have to get their attention."

"How? I don't see anything out there."

"It's hard to spot in the daytime. That's what makes it perfect. They're literally hiding in plain sight."

Georgette didn't look convinced, but she sat down along with the others. Except for Brian. He didn't appear to be all that tired and stood guard with his rifle. He hadn't said a word since they started off, which Keo found impressive. He was expecting the teenager to fight him every inch of the way, but the kid had instead stayed mum.

Keo took out the small compact with the paint and mirror from one of his pockets. He twisted the lid, breaking it loose, then made sure he caught the sunlight just right and flicked the mirror back and forth.

"What are you doing?" Georgette asked.

"I'm signaling them," Keo said.

"Is that some kind of Morse code?"

"Yes."

"What if no one there knows Morse code?"

Zachary will know.

Keo didn't know why he believed that, he just did. Zachary was one of those guys who was born to live out here in the wilds. The fact that he had spent two nights hiding in the ground while the creatures roamed above him convinced Keo the man was either suicidal or just really skilled. And a guy like that, he thought, probably knew Morse code.

Hopefully.

"Even if no one knows Morse code, I'll still have gotten their attention," Keo said. "So sit down and relax."

"I can't," Georgette said. "I've been walking through the woods for half a day. We're all hungry and thirsty, and I'm starting to think Brian may be right about taking one of the trucks…."

Keo ignored her and continued signaling. Even if he was wrong about Zachary, at least they would know someone was out here. That might be enough for Allie to send someone to check—

There.

The sunlight reflected back something in the distance—a response.

Georgette saw it and hurried over. "What's that?"

"The island," Keo said.

"So, it worked?"

"Yes."

"What does it say?"

He read the flickering light, stringing the letters together. Finally, he smiled.

"Shouldn't you be dead, San Diego?" the message read.

CHAPTER 19

"How is he?" Keo asked, looking down at Norris's sleeping form. He had never seen the old-timer looking so peaceful in his life.

"They really worked on him," Allie said. "I didn't think he'd survive past the night, but he proved me wrong. He's stubborn. Which I guess is why you two get along so well."

"That's one theory."

They were in the back room of her houseboat, with Norris snoring on one of the lower bunk beds. Two open windows allowed plenty of light inside, along with a nice and surprisingly cool breeze this afternoon.

"He'll be mostly fine with a lot of rest," Allie said. "And I mean a lot of rest. Zachary told me you guys were headed down south to New Orleans."

"That was the plan."

"That's not going to happen if you want him to live past the week."

He nodded, because that was his best-case scenario anyway. Norris's appearance had been barely okay two nights ago, but the morning after he looked worse than half-dead.

"And what about you?" Allie said. "You were actually good looking when you were last here. What happened?"

He grinned and didn't want to imagine what he actually looked like at the moment. Zachary and Shorty had done a double take when they came to pick him and the kids up in one of the pontoon boats. The blood still clung to the fabric of his shirt, and his face was probably black and purple. His nose was certainly a different shade than his skin color, and the long bandage stretching from the middle of his cheek to his temple probably didn't improve his looks any.

"You should see the other guy," he said.

"I bet," Allie said. "That was a hell of a fight back there. I was listening to it all day. Then when I thought it was over, you went at it again all night. What was that about?"

He told her about the men in hazmat suits and saw the look on her face. He guessed that was probably the same expression he had given Georgette when she told him about the same men last night.

"Are you serious?" Allie said, when he was finished.

"As a heart attack."

"You have any idea who they were, or what they wanted?"

"They didn't stick around to tell us in the morning, and we didn't feel like going out there to find out when it was still dark."

"What about the bloodsuckers? Did they just...ignore them?"

"I don't know. I just know that they were out there and I didn't see a single creature around them."

"That's..." She shook her head, speechless. "Jesus Christ. As if we don't have enough to worry about."

Hazmat suits. Gas masks.

What the hell's going on out there in the rest of the world?

"What about the kids?" he asked.

"You took a big risk bringing them here."

"It wasn't much of a risk. They're three teenagers and a scared twenty-something without adult supervision."

"With automatic weapons."

"Just the one."

"One's all it takes." Then, softening a bit, "Maybe you're right. They seemed harmless enough. More hungry than anything."

"They're not the only ones," he said, just as his stomach growled.

Allie smiled. "She must be gorgeous, huh?"

"'She'?"

"This girl you're all hot and bothered to finally get to after all these months."

He smiled, but didn't answer.

"I thought so," she said.

AFTERWARD, HE ATE in the dining room of the houseboat by himself. He was starving and wolfed down the plate of fried fish and sucked out everything from the fish heads, eyeballs and all.

Georgette, Brian, and the other two girls were busy walking around the island's limited space, meeting the residents who called this place home. In the couple of times he saw them, they looked both impressed and frightened, and he couldn't tell if they were making plans to spend the rest of their lives here or leave the first chance they got. Not that whatever they decided mattered to him anymore. He had his own path, and it wasn't up north.

Allie came out of the back room while he was still eating. "Jesus, it's a good thing the lake's full of fish."

He grinned, feeling slightly sheepish at the pile of bones on his plate.

Allie pushed aside some of the dishes and unfolded a map between them. "So," she said, pointing at Downey Creek Lake and Robertson Park. "You're here. And this is where you want to go. New Orleans."

Keo took a moment between bites to trace his progress ever since leaving Earl's house. He saw the surrounding area for the first time and now suddenly understood why he felt as if he had been blindly running around in the woods for the last few months.

Because he had been.

He and Norris had tracked about thirty kilometers since the gunfight from Earl's house. It had seemed like an eternity, and he was certain they had gone farther south than that. But no, according to the map, they were no closer to New Orleans. The city was still a distant blip from his current position, more than 400 kilometers away.

"I'm off course," Keo said.

"No kidding," Allie said. "How long were you in those woods?"

"A long time. We must have been going in circles for God knows how long. Jesus."

"No map?"

"No."

"Well, you were being hunted like mangy dogs day and night, and neither one of you are from the area, so..." She put her finger on New Orleans. "Anyway, your bright idea was to launch from Orleans?"

"That was the plan."

"Why?"

"What do you mean?"

She traced the map as she talked. "NOLA is southeast. But Lake Charles is southwest, and you'll be saving probably a hundred miles of travel if you went there instead. There are other benefits to Lake Charles. Plenty of marinas to find a boat that'll fit your needs, and you'd be much closer to Texas when you finally did launch."

Keo stared at the map for a moment. "You're right. Lake Charles was always the better choice."

"There's also Lake Dulcet before that. Smaller casino town, but like Charles, it joins up with Lake Beaufont through a series of river veins. From there, it's an easy trip into the Gulf of Mexico. See?"

"I thought you were a divorce lawyer before all of this?"

She rolled her eyes. "I can read a map, Keo."

"That helps, too."

She folded the map back up and handed it to him. "Have you been monitoring FEMA?"

"In the first few months after everything happened. Why?"

She walked over to a cabinet and came back with a radio. "Then you were probably like us. We kept waiting for the state or government to tell us everything was all right, that we could finally head back home. Of course, it never happened."

The radio was old and beaten, but it powered on just fine.

He wasn't surprised by the lack of anything other than static coming through the speakers.

"A while back—maybe four months ago?—we finally picked up something by accident," Allie said. "Zachary was playing with the radio and he happened to land on the FEMA band."

"FEMA is the U.S. government."

"I know. But it wasn't the government. Someone else was tapping into the frequency. A group of people from Beaufont Lake, on a place called Song Island. They were telling other survivors to go to them, that they had electricity, food, and shelter. They also told us something we already knew—that the creatures won't cross bodies of water. It was a recorded message playing in a loop. Twenty-four seven. Come to Song Island. Shelter. Food. Electricity."

"If it was on a twenty-four seven loop, that means they really do have a power source."

"Or they did," Allie said. "The message stopped. Just like that—one day it wasn't there anymore."

"What happened?"

"We don't know."

"You never went there to find out if what they were offering was real?"

"It was tempting. We definitely considered packing up and going there. We even took a vote, but in the end, most people decided to stay here. We don't have a lot here, but we have enough, and we can always find more in the surrounding shoreline. Out there..." She shook her head. "You know how dangerous it is."

He nodded. "Understandable. Why take the chance?"

"Not everyone voted to stay. Some wanted to go, and they did, about a week after we first heard the message. There were seven of them."

"Did they make it?"

"I don't know. We haven't heard from them since. That in itself is a bad sign, because they promised to contact us once they got there using whatever was broadcasting the message." She walked back to the shelf and put the radio away. "Zachary was friends with some of the people who went. I think he wanted to go too, but stayed because he thought the others here needed him more. That was then, though. We've gotten into a routine, and I think we can afford to let him go now."

"What are you saying, Allie?"

"Unless you want to wait for Norris to heal up, you'll have to go out there by yourself. I'm saying you don't have to. If you ask Zachary, I think he'd jump at the chance to go with you. I know he wants to find out what happened to his friends, and he believes the answers are on Song Island." She sat back down. "I'd hate to lose him, but I know it's killing him that he doesn't know."

Keo looked over at the door into the back room. "I have to talk to Norris first."

"BACK IN MY day, you whippersnappers didn't leave the old folks to die on a boat," Norris said. "You had the decency to dump them into a home. Kids these days."

"Stop your bitching," Keo said. "Besides, I would drag you along, but Allie says you'd be dead within a day."

"She a doctor?"

"Ex-lawyer."

Norris grunted. "I have a couple of rules in life: Never trust a guy with a gun pointed at you, and never trust a lawyer."

"She's a divorce lawyer."

"Even worse."

Keo smiled. "Admit it. You want to stay. This place will extend your life by a few more years. I read somewhere that a steady diet of fish is supposed to be good for your longevity."

Norris peered at him with surprising seriousness. "You really good with this, kid? Me staying here?"

"You're only going to slow me down, old-timer. I promised Gillian, and I'm already way overdue. I have to make up time before she finds another guy."

"That your way of trying to make me feel better?"

"There's nothing for you to feel bad about."

"Yeah, well…" He let it trail off and didn't say anything for a moment. Finally, he said, "I'm assuming this isn't a two-way trip."

"Not if I can help it."

He sighed. "I gotta admit, it's not a bad way to waste however many years I have left. Of course, I'm not sure I'm ever going to get used to sleeping on the ocean."

"It's not really an ocean."

"Ocean, lake, whatever," Norris said, looking down at his bare feet on the sun-drenched foredeck of Allie's houseboat. "I always figured I'd end up in a lot of places when I left Orlando, but a floating boat in the middle of a lake was definitely not one of them."

"That's what makes life interesting. Surprises."

"Says the guy with a pretty girl waiting for him on a beach somewhere."

If she's still alive, Keo thought, but said instead, "You wouldn't want to keep traipsing around the country with me, anyway. It's way too hot out there for an old coot."

"You got that right."

"I'm frankly shocked you're still alive."

Norris chuckled. "You and me both, kid. You and me both."

The ex-cop looked better in the sunlight, though Keo still didn't trust him not to fall down at any moment. He had struggled out of bed and walked the length of the boat before anyone had even spotted him. Keo still couldn't see Norris's bruised and battered body beneath his pants and a white T-shirt, and he didn't have to. It was written all over the older man's face and in the careful way he moved every muscle, as if just breathing hurt.

Keo knew a little bit about that himself. His broken nose had been giving him trouble the last two days while he waited for Norris to wake up. His side still throbbed when he walked, but it was really the itching along the left portion of his face that was getting on his nerves.

"Anyway, you shouldn't be on your feet," Keo said.

"If a doctor had said that, I might have listened."

"I think Allie knows what she's talking about."

"Probably." He looked up at the clear, sunny sky and blinked against the sun. "How did I get here, anyway?"

"You don't remember?"

"Nope."

"Zachary and Shorty carried you. You've been asleep for

two days."

"No wonder I feel so good." He paused for a moment, then, "Riggs would never leave Murtaugh behind."

"Yeah, well, you were already too old for this shit when all of this began. At this point, you're pretty much stinking up the joint."

Norris grunted before grinning at him. "So, this Allie. She pretty or what? No one was there when I woke up."

"She's definitely a looker. But I don't think she goes for old guys."

"Of course not," Norris frowned. "Why should my luck improve all of a sudden?" Then he beamed, looking half his age all of a sudden. "I can't believe we're still alive. *Dae*-fucking-*bak*, kid."

Keo looked out at the glistening lake and smiled. *"Daebak*, old-timer."

"You sure you're gonna be fine out there without me?"

"I'll get by."

"I don't doubt it. You're a survivor, kid. This kind of world was made for people like you, not old farts like me."

"Is that what that smell is?"

Norris grunted. "Smartass."

Keo grinned. "We never got around to grabbing a Blu-ray of *Lethal Weapon*."

"Nope. We'll put that on the to-do list when we meet up again."

"What was it called, anyway?"

"What's that?"

"The sequel to *Lethal Weapon*."

Norris chuckled. *"Lethal Weapon 2*. They called the third and fourth one *Lethal Weapon 3* and *Lethal Weapon 4*, respectively."

"Not very creative of them," Keo said.

"Nah, they sorta blew their load with the first movie," Norris said. "The first sequel was pretty good, though…"

EPILOGUE

"TO ANY SURVIVORS out there, if you're hearing this, you are not alone. There are things you need to know about our enemy—these creatures of the night, these ghouls. They are not invincible, and they have weaknesses other than sunlight. One: you can kill them with silver. Stab them, shoot them, or cut them with any silver weapon, and they will die. Two: they will not cross bodies of water. An island, a boat—get to anything that can separate you from land. Three: some ultraviolet light has proven effective, but flashlights and lightbulbs with UV don't seem to have any effect. We don't know why, so use this information with caution. If you're hearing this message, you are not alone. Stay strong, stay smart, and adapt. We owe it to those we've lost to keep fighting, to never give up. Good luck."

85647470R00148

Made in the USA
Columbia, SC
20 December 2017